TENGO SED

Literature and
Medicine Series

STATEMENT OF PURPOSE: The art of writing and the science of medicine offer very different approaches to some of the most intense and mysterious human experiences. The Literature and Medicine series, jointly sponsored by the University of New Mexico Press and the University of New Mexico's Health Sciences Center, brings together these two ways of understanding. Comprising fiction and creative nonfiction, the series showcases stories that explore the nature of health and healing and the texture of the experience of illness.

ADVISORY EDITORS: Elizabeth Hadas, Frank Huyler, M.D., and David P. Sklar, M.D.

TENGO SED *a novel*

JAMES FLEMING

University of New Mexico Press ✚ Albuquerque

Library of Congress Cataloging-in-Publication Data
Fleming, James, 1962–
Tengo sed : a novel / James Fleming.
p. cm. — (Literature and medicine series)
ISBN 978-0-8263-4953-8 (pbk. : alk. paper)
1. Hospitals—Emergency services—Fiction. I. Title.
PS3606.L464T46 2010
813'.6—dc22
2010005181

For the Mulloolys,
all of them.

Mother died today.

—Albert Camus, *The Stranger*

ACKNOWLEDGMENTS

I have been writing for years and have never been able to pull off a complete work. The fact that this is complete is a large debt. I thank Janet Bailey for her reading and frank criticism. None of this would have happened without David Sklar, author of *La Clínica* and then chair of our department, who created the environment in emergency medicine where would-be writers could flourish. I will never forget Beth Hadas, who not only threw out the first edition, but was far more than instrumental in making the current edition stand. My greatest thanks, however, will always be to Frank Huyler, who understands writing better than anyone I have met. I read his *Blood of Strangers* before I came to UNM. Now I know that he is why I came to UNM.

Lastly, to my wife Anne Kortsch Fleming, who had it been up to her I never would have gone to medical school. She always said, "Just write, Jim." Thanks for believing—your magnum opus is yet to come. And my kids, nothing outdoes them except when we are together eating cheeseburgers on pillows.

I alone am responsible for the content. It might be easy to take the content as criticism, but those who do will be greatly mistaken.

PRELUDE TO MORNING

I never thought I would know how long a day was. Now I do. Down to the minute. My Jolly Rancher melting away in my mouth at 5:31, followed by a slurp of coffee. Good morning, New Mexico!

I have been up all night with the sick and the lame. They have tubes in their mouths. I don't. I look at them. They are too tired to roll over and look away.

Day creeps into day. The movement is invisible. Sleep ordinarily breaks the monotony of our lives, gives a false sense of renewal, but really we are there all along. My duties will end with rounds, a presentation of all the patients in the ICU, a good morning and farewell all at once.

While most of the world thinks of rounds as something circular or a cut of steak, here in the medical world it is actually linear. We take the flesh and line it up (that is when the intern updates the list of patients), prepare it (that is when the intern pre-rounds), talk about it (that is when the intern presents the patient), make a plan (this is when the intern learns humility), and then execute it (this is when the patient's head, with any luck, stays attached and we learn something). This is called rounds. Rounds are a sacred undertaking, a daily undertaking, a stand-until-you-drop undertaking, and then you come back up to the surface for more. *What was I saying? Which system of the body—the holy five: Neuro, Pulmonary, Cardiovascular, FEN/GI/GU and Heme/ID—was I on?* And you keep going. Your mouth moving too fast over words you're too tired to say. And the wind blows, and it does not matter what kind of hellfire your boss breathes forth or how starched his pantaloons are, nor what brand of coffee he guzzles before he spits on you. You will push through and find yourself on the other side of the day. You are an Israelite in the middle of a psalm. And morning in its mercy always comes.

1

That is the short of a night as an intern, but really it's much longer, like watching one of those fat drugstore candles burning while you are thinking, "This thing will certainly go out before it burns to the end of the wick" . . . until you wake up with the dresser on fire and no one in your arms. It's just you and the Trauma-Surgical ICU, in short, fire, worry, nausea, and the sickest patients in New Mexico, everything the A bomb missed: rollover accidents, stabbings, third degree burns, gunshot wounds, hangings, and simply freezing to the ice when they get too drunk to walk. They all gather together, strangers in a common fate who never meet, never walk from one bed to the next like in *A Farewell to Arms* and say "Hey, I'm José. How's your leg?"

It's quiet except for the ventilators, the IV pumps, the coffee maker, and the chatter of the residents and nurses. The visitors are silent, looking at a family member separated in space and time by the instrumentation of modern medicine, and they feel like astronauts experiencing the loss of gravity for the first time. It's hard to sit down in those rooms.

My role here is very unclear. I am Hovercraft, always around, always feeling on the edge. Being an intern entitles you to a questionable shell of reality. There are the hours. There are the voices: "*Go away Hovercraft but be near, be out of sight, but be a whistle's blow away. I might let you do a chest tube, though I might not, but don't drink too much coffee—in case I get an inkling of generosity, your hand might shake—but don't fall asleep either, it's hard to do a chest tube when your head's up your ass.*" To a surgeon you have just been given a form of encouragement. But like the *Rolling Stone* issue with Bob Dylan on the cover boasting an exclusive interview in which he finally reveals himself, you are sure to be disappointed. No Bob Dylan, and *well, we decided to do the chest tube ourselves. It was emergent, Hovercraft. Go pre-round.*

Tonight the team is reduced to three: the urology intern, Harry, who is going to cover four other surgical services tonight, the senior surgical resident, and me. The surgical resident is waiting for his relief, two more surgical residents who do what is called night float. Harry and I are waiting for dawn.

Harry's and my relationship is a relationship of place. Sometimes relationships of place are the best ones. You come together briefly for a common cause, love simply, and part not under the force of a conscious decision but because life goes on.

I call Harry Fivehead because, even with a whole head of hair, his forehead is so large and prominent that . . . well, it is impossible that it could be just fore; it has to be a fivehead. He is like a nomad in the ICU, ranging wherever he chooses, leading his camel next to my bare feet during rounds. He always tells me: "Those who are really smart hardly need to talk; they radiate competence, while those who really are not, need to quote studies and repeatedly revalidate their competence for all to see."

I tell him that might be, but there is another level of silence where I dwell, and you can't find it at your local public library.

When I told Fivehead I was a crack baby, he told me he was a Thalidomide baby. When I told him I really was not, he took me under his wing anyway. He has a face only a mother could love, but how could I not love Fivehead?

"I have to go check on my assignments. They're paging me for report," he says.

Luckily, the nurses in this ICU go in on Starbucks coffee, which I don't dare brew without their consent. I plan on drinking coffee at full strength until I die. It goes well with the abundance of crackers they stock beneath the pot. And since I gained weight in medical school, I have decided to go on a crackers only diet. The idea: you can eat as many crackers as you like, but that's all you can eat.

My favorite at this time of day is the unit clerk, Hankie. I peek out of the break room to see if she has arrived, but I don't see her. She usually sits up front and guards the door. She is pale, like a ghost, with medium-cut gray hair and swollen ankles. She hates interns because we are always either changing our minds about our orders or adding new ones, usually as the result of a nurse's suggestion. She is sixty-two but can sneer and punch down charts with the youngest of them. *"Can't you ever make up your mind, intern? Can't you think for yourself and not let those old male sluts of nurses tell you what to do? I'm sick of all your fucking orders."* Bang. The chart is pinned under her forearm. She growls, daring you to order anything ever again.

I sit down, drink the ancient coffee, nibble on a saltine from the holy land and look around the break room. Someone has left the *New York Times* on the table. I leaf through it. Iraq is not going well. A small group of red-scarfed women are mourning on the front page. I wonder why the family of Room 6 is not mourning likewise. Somehow the breathing tube and the regular sound of the respirator reassure them like a radio turned down low.

2

"What are you doing, Hovercraft?" It is Trauma Attending Pizza at the door. "I suppose you know everything about BiVent?"

Human relationships have many beginnings.

I'm an ER intern. I'm working in the trauma-surgical ICU, or TSI for short, for the month. Some relationships start out with kind remarks and simple wishes, but quickly get complicated, layered, and then fall down three flights of stairs. I was down at the bottom of the stairs when I first looked up at Trauma Attending Pizza. He was my boss. He was everything I was not: arrogant, steeled, and facile. He was both father figure and my little brother, and I could never get unglued from between the two. I physically dreaded seeing him, avoided him if I could, but I never could escape rounds. Then he had me pinned down on the ironing board, and I could see the iron coming, lifted in the sky. At bottom he was just a punk from the Rockies, nothing special, nothing to pull your hair out about, but on the fields of arrogance and fatigue, we hated each other clearly, dearly, and all the way down the three flights of stairs.

TA Pizza was almost like Achilles. After languishing and sulking on his ship in a small community ER on the coast of California, he had struck out boldly for a program in New York City called Shock Trauma Live. There he trained as a trauma intensivist, sorted the living and the dead, and came to believe in the power of scoring systems and criteria for nearly every ailment. There was the Well's criterion for predicting deep vein thrombosis, the Canadian head rule, the Nexus neck rule, the Ottawa knee and ankle rules, the San Francisco syncope rule, a rule for heroism, and an unpublished rule for getting as much cunt.as possible. He came to New Mexico on a white horse wearing sunglasses, ready to amaze, hobnob, and to admonish. He was the only non-surgeon on Trauma Surgery Island. It was a new paradigm UNM was trying: have an intensivist manage the trauma ICU and let the surgeons do surgery. He was an experiment, a dog on a leash, and he knew it. He never lost that wild sense of being on edge and of having something to prove. He knew the literature, and he was ready to fight with anyone on rounds. He loved the sport of medicine and liked to think he brought down big game in the trauma room. But still he had his weakness and five words made him uneasy: "I'm not a trauma surgeon."

He woke up every morning hoping his fortunes had changed, but no matter how many times he looked in the mirror, he did not see a trauma surgeon. He was almost like Achilles, but instead he was an intensivist.

He thought about returning for a surgical residency, but medical training was very unforgiving. There was no partial credit for having previously gone down another path. It was back to the beginning. The long hours. The endless nights. The year without entering the OR before finally being coached through a gallbladder removal and not being trusted, and with good reason.

He was not married. But the money was already so good and the shine in the residents' eyes was nearly blinding. Yet he longed for those battlefields of blood, even dreamed about going to South Africa, where machete injuries were at an all time high.

The year at Shock Trauma Live had been the most fulfilling of his short career. He hardly left the hospital. He slept where he wanted and ate fast food to sustain himself, then yelled, "Roll him!" out of a near sleep.

When the year ended, he found a job in the trauma ICU in New Mexico, but like most doctors at the end of training, realized he was supposed to do something else. Instead of doing surgery, he presided and worked the atmosphere, made the rain come and let the sun shine. He was an attending in the widest sense of the word, a weather man, the coming storm, an intensivist.

It's 4 o'clock in the afternoon. The sky blue. Trauma Attending Tickle is walking in the basement of the place. In fact, he is at the foot of the bed of a fresh trauma. It's like fresh vegetables. He is talking to Trauma Attending Pizza. It's like the two of them are at a market deciding how to prepare the squash. Pizza wants it with butter and chives according to a new study out of Australia. TA Tickle, who can do surgery, wants it raw.

"Why don't you get yourself back upstairs and let a surgeon take care of this," Tickle finally says.

3

A blue Chrysler minivan pulls into a gas station off I-70. The gas station, which was built with a restaurant back in the sixties, has recently been renamed a Travel Center. In addition to breath mints and cigarettes, you can get about every food that is bad for you. But this early it is pancakes, warm buttery pancakes pierced through with blueberries that land in your gut like a baseball in a glove. The syrup drips down your throat for hours afterward.

The Kennedys, one then two, climb out of the minivan and unstrap their two children from the backseat. George has driven all night and particularly enjoyed the traces of blue as the sun came back into the sky.

"What are we having for breakfast Maddie?" he says to his youngest daughter. She is now four.

"Pancakes!"

"Maddie, you have been taught well."

The Kennedys are on a cross-country trip that will end at Sea World in San Diego. George likes to save money by driving at night. The car becomes like a floating motel, so to speak, and then he feels like he is getting his pancakes for free in the morning. The only problem is the lack of sleep. This he solves by having his wife drive for a few hours in the morning.

George owns a restaurant back in Jersey and serves what he believes is the best cheeseburger in the country. It starts with a toasted semmel, a kind of Bavarian hard roll that warms up crisp on the outside and warm and flaky on the inside. The meat is Jersey beef made fresh daily and cooks up evenly, without pockets of ice like its frozen counterparts, on a charcoal grill. On this he spoons stewed onions and tops it with aged Wisconsin cheddar. The smoke rises luxuriously, and the butter is applied liberally. People talk about a heart attack on a bun, but George always insists that if you could not eat his cheeseburger, you would have a heart attack from sheer, buttery lust.

He agrees he has a thing or two to learn about pancakes. So every December he packs up the wife and kids and heads out across America on a "business trip" to see what the rest of the country is cooking. He does not know what he will do next year when Maddie starts kindergarten but, "Here's for living in the moment," he thinks and slams the driver's side door.

Maddie runs.

"Maddie," he yells.

But rather than being scared, Maddie turns around and impishly cries, "Pancakes."

For no good reason George's guard goes down. He turns his attention to Edith. Maddie stands at the base of a parking block when suddenly a black pickup truck turns. George yells again, now in alarm. Maddie jumps to the sidewalk and runs to the door of the restaurant, clean and free, a little Jersey girl with brown pigtails and a T-shirt that reads, "Real diners don't sell T-shirts." Subtitle: Kennedy's Café. She smiles.

"Wait there," he calls.

Now comes the special part of this blue Chrysler minivan. Half of the back seat has been taken out to make room. Like when Jesus said to his disciples, "I go now so that I may make room." There is a lift controlled by a switch inside the door. It is simple: the brown button brings the lift down and the green one makes it ascend. The only trick is you have to duck pretty deep to fit over Edith's chair and under the ceiling, but George does not have the money to buy a regulation-size handicapped van.

Under the darkened ceiling, Edith is much simpler. Edith is twisted. She drools and keeps her eyes wide open looking past you. She is pure being. George can see the long days ahead, always pushing the wheelchair well into his fifties, sixties, maybe seventies from tourist town to tourist town. And he can see all the people watching because it is a free freak show to go with their ice cream cones. You cannot blame them. You cannot get sick of looking at Edith. No one knows who she is because she does not recognize or answer to her name. Every day the tree falls in the wilderness in her presence and does not make a sound. So much for philosophy. Yet she can eat pancakes with the best of them, once her mouth habituates to the fact it has a load to swallow. Prior to that there is a lot of spillage.

Although she is only four, Maddie has risen to the occasion. She calls Edith sissy, and that will never change until the day she dies.

Judith has the hardest time. She can never picture herself having a mentally retarded daughter distorted by cerebral palsy. It is like having expected a Van Gogh and being given a Jackson Pollock instead. It makes no sense, and Judith is sure appearances matter.

But now it is pancake time, and George remembers this Travel Center's pancakes well, right down to the crisp fringe of the cake.

4.

There are no windows to watch the twilight. One just understands that twilight kneels down and belches out night.

The night floats arrive, which means it is dinner time. I hide my preference for crackers behind a green chile cheeseburger, fries, and a cherry coke. There isn't much point in being healthy. Food is your lover as long as you can get it. Scorn and, worse, pity might be your meal for the rest of the night. I page Fivehead to join us.

I am on with Crystal and Geoff, either of whom could make your asshole bleed without putting their finger in it. We process to the cafeteria. Doctors don't walk. Fivehead comes shortly after like the caboose of a train.

"Thanks for saving me," he says to me. "I thought I was never going to get out of that room."

"What was the issue?" Geoff says, leaning into the taco bar.

"Oh, nothing. Nothing I couldn't handle," Fivehead says, slightly taken aback by his intrusion.

"Then it wasn't an issue?" Geoff says, soothing as he prods.

"*Issue* was your word."

"You said, 'Thanks for saving me.' I assumed there was something happening in the doctor-patient relationship. In other words, an issue."

"No, it involved a family member, a question."

"Good, a question, not an issue. Like should I take the sour cream now that the salad has fallen into it?" He has processed down the bar and is ladling salsa over his soft shells.

Fivehead's pager goes off. Again he is saved.

Geoff smiles in amusement. He says nothing more about the issue question. He does not look back. He has stopped on Maslow's hierarchy; lost in industry, he sees nothing to gain by moving on to trust or self-discovery.

I bite into a fry and listen to Crystal and Geoff talk about their evaluations tomorrow. I am in another world, out of reach of the signal tower. I want to talk about Bob Dylan on the cover of the *Rolling Stone*, but I am an anomaly.

I remember once listening to an interview in which he says there are things he would like to do but can't. The interviewer laughs, thinking of Dylan's wealth. But the interviewer doesn't know what to say when Dylan says he'd like to go to medical school. "A surgeon who saves my life on the highway is the man I'm going to admire." That's the thing about Dylan that people don't understand. He's always thinking of possibilities. He would have made a good surgeon. He could shut them all up.

Crystal is in her late twenties, the daughter of a surgeon. She grew up in a cold town in northern Wisconsin along Lake Superior. She is half Asian and half Caucasian, a beautiful girl with an easy smile and straight dark hair. She has the nervous habit of always checking her cell phone. Or maybe she is looking for a way out, the call that will drive her out of surgery and into art. But artists, like surgeons, aren't called. Still the rumor is that she studied music in her undergraduate days and is an excellent flutist.

Geoff, strictly speaking, is OCD, a perfectionist, and a tyrant with soft hands and excellent technical skills. Raised in the Deep South, he is prone to tantrums, which are overlooked, and his racial slurs trumped by operating acumen. He has the smuggest smile this side of Texas and people initially always 100 percent of the time think that he is an easygoing gentleman. But in reality, with his red hair, freckles, and his deep dark side, he is like a Howdy Doody doll ready to ape-shit explode. You just have to pull the strings. To change an antibiotic behind his back you would have thought you took off his mother's underpants. We all make fun of him but at some level are afraid of him because in the world we are living in, his skills and knowledge matter, and we all buy into the theory that the knowledge of taking care of patients is power. It doesn't matter if you just met Jesus on the road to Emmaus.

Crystal looks at me. "You're looking wide awake tonight."

"Don't I always?" I say, hopefully.

"No, sometimes you look old, and those French fries aren't going to help you."

To be a surgeon you have to like throwing people on their backs to see if they will get up.

There is something I like about Crystal, but it might just boil down to the youth I've lost and her unambiguous grasp of this reality we share.

"I just had my eyebrows waxed," I say.

"Really?" Crystal says like I had done something great.

Geoff looks at me like a fucking hospital. "No plastic surgery on my service," he says. "Your eyebrows?" He shakes his head.

Our meal is finished. Fivehead never returns.

"Let's head back to the *Titanic*," Geoff says. It is common terminology used by all the residents. The unit is like a ship ultimately doomed, but every morning at dawn we sail forth.

Geoff is throbbing, packed full of energy. As always, I trail him up the hall. I never seem to be able to walk step for step with him. But this is common. When a team of doctors and medical students parade down the hall, you can be certain of their rank by their place in line. Age does not matter. Incurable disease does not count. Length of coat is practically irrelevant. As you advance in training you walk faster. It is amazing—an athletic hierarchy.

Geoff slams the steel plate, opening the *Titanic*. He is in charge. Crystal wanders off to do yoga in the call room. I go back to the *New York Times*. A fresh pot of coffee is brewing, blowing off a thin wisp of steam.

I look down at my trauma pager thinking that if I look at it, it won't go off. Of course, I look away and off it goes.

34 year old male hanging, failed intubation, cric'd, reads the text message. Soon we will be reconvening, Crystal out of her trance, Geoff to resume power, and me to record the history and physical of the resuscitation through my coffee dreams.

Dressed in a blue gown, purple gloves, and an orange mask shield, Geoff folds his arms and smiles vacantly like a bobblehead trauma doll. I open the packet of papers and stand at the foot of the bed with the difficult airway cart as my desk. Crystal sways, relaxed, still chanting inwardly but with her hands firm.

A purple head with disheveled brown hair and opened lips is the first thing through the door. Next is the neck with a tube sticking out of it, followed by the enormous half-dressed chest. The ER resident at the head of the bed counts out the transfer as the paramedic continues to bag. One of the ER techs takes over on compressions. His hair is two colors, gold and black, and gelled down the middle so it does not move as he pumps the man's chest. The man is purple clear down to his nipples.

His hair is greasy like he has spent many days of sporadic activity followed by long periods of sleep before he reached his conclusion. His hands are still pink but swollen. The nicotine stain between his index and middle finger is spreading out like a sail.

"I know he smoked," I say, like an idiot savant filling out my form. "But did he drink or use drugs?"

"Hovercraft, shut up," Geoff says. He is politeness itself for the moment.

Tickle makes his way out of his private quarters to the head of the bed. "Stop compressions," he barks. He shouts to the housekeeper in the doorway to stop her mopping. Tickle looks at the tube sticking out of the neck.

"Give me a scalpel," he says.

The man is big and Tickle cuts into the fat of his neck. He follows the tube into a dead end of yellow fat right above the breast bone.

"The goddamn tube isn't even in the trachea," he says.

Geoff is looking off in the distance for the iceberg which will suddenly upend the trauma room, but Tickle knows it is a simple mistake, less glorious than the lights and sirens that have parted the evening rush hour traffic of Albuquerque. The purple man has been without oxygen for at least twenty minutes, every second since he was cut down. Probably longer. Tickle pronounces him. We leave the ER resident, Mick, to take care of the body. The housekeeper moves back in. It is 18:12. I want to go home.

5

Our Lady of Guadalupe is very important in New Mexico, but so is the Gadfly. The Gadfly is an ICU nurse in her mid-twenties. Some people you meet and they just pass. Others hold your attention for years.

Early in her shift, the Gadfly is all business and has little to do with small talk. But even then I glamorize her and try to see things through her eyes. I feel the poverty of my medical knowledge next to hers.

"I can't believe this guy is still alive," she says. "Shot six times in the belly and back."

"How are you?" I say.

"I don't know," she says. She lifts her styrofoam cup of coffee. "The coffee's fresh. You ought to go get some."

I never turn down a cup of coffee, but for a moment I stare at the numbers of Bed 3.

Bed 3 is a twenty-two-year-old Spanish boy left for dead in the South Valley. Carlos López's story didn't make you cry but seeing the overflowing gathering of family and friends standing around his glass doors in different-colored alligator-skin cowboy boots made you wonder. Stick a white guy shot six times, the last time in the back, in Bed 3 and you would be hard pressed to draw a crowd of three. White people were afraid of their connection to each other and sought solitude like the Lone Ranger, masked in the face of death.

Yet here there was so much love and honor for Carlos López, whose face was chiseled by acne and poverty and whose limbs bore the track marks of a middle-aged man's heroin addiction, and Carlos fought blindly from a deep well of life to grab back his ten square feet of the South Valley. He would plant string beans there and smoke a Marlboro in the pissing bee-loud glade.

Carlos was a master of contradictions. Tattooed over his heart was the simple word *Madre,* yet he treated the women he saw in the street like they were nothing but whores and also-rans. Still take the Virgin Mary's name in vain and Carlos would be at your throat. "Don't you fucking ever piss on my mother's or my fucking mother's mother's name." It came out with more profanity than the other guy could lace gold foil around Our Lady of Guadalupe, but to Carlos it was honor. And he breathed honor every time he shot up and let the compelling dream of sincerity and the compelling fix of necessity grab hold of him, and no one could say that Carlos López was not free. He owned the whole pissing South Valley.

Until he became mortal and was shot four times at close range, then twice as he was running away. He could not even remember what the argument was about, but he knew he was bleeding and the black pickup truck with its high buffed chrome was pulling away. A terrible loneliness took hold of him. He could see no one.

He woke up in the ambulance bulleting down the avenue. He could hear only the echo of the screeching sirens. There was a burning in his gut and the taste of blood in his mouth. They unloaded him. There were people standing all around under bright slanted lights.

"Am I going to die?" he said. They were the only words he could come up with. No one said anything to him. They had him back in the hall. Doors broke open. "I'm not going to pissing die," he swore.

Rosaries were said for Carlos in cluttered waiting rooms. Two times they called him lost and another time homeward bound. But he was no Simon and Garfunkel. He was Nuevo Mexicano, the purest American blood. His ancestors reached back before the time of the queer Mayflower and its delicate landing at Plymouth Rock. His ancestors wore chain mail and rode black horses and had tasted glory in the hot noon sun.

So Carlos hung on. Made it out of the operating room. Holed up in Bed 3. Loaded up with chest tubes, pressors, and fluids, he would come down off the mountain like Jesus and reveal his wounds, and those who believed would be transfixed. He would be a sign of God's vigilance, and then he would have his vengeance.

6

Geoff is looking up X-rays on the computer. He is lining up his ducks for the next day in case he gets to operate. He has a passion for knowing everything about the patients who are left in his care. He can operate on a moment's notice. He has no case of the nerves like his Hovercraft. Prickly but exact with a scalpel is his trademark and he can sew with the oldest ladies of the oldest knitting club. Geoff really is the ideal resident to leave in charge. He can make decisions in an instant and not second guess himself. In trauma you not only have to be able to take care of the patient at hand, you have to be ready for the next without a thought for the first.

I am coming around the station with my styrofoam cup of coffee to see if there is anything I can do when the trauma pager goes off.

MVA rollover. 44 year old female. Unrestrained with altered level of consciousness.

Again we make our way to the trauma room, but this time Crystal has beat us there. She is already gowned. Overhead you can hear the helicopter burning the air above the landing pad. I think they should pipe the MASH theme song into the trauma room whenever that helicopter flies.

"This one is live," Crystal says. "Hovercraft, get a chest tube ready."

I stand transiently paralyzed, like I did so many times that first year, and watch the ER resident Laurie Ann at the head of the bed preparing for intubation. "I want 30 of Etomidate and 100 of roc ready," she says to the nurse. Meanwhile the respiratory therapist has joined the gathering and is setting up the ventilator.

"I have to work fast. I have to work fast," I keep saying in my head as I slowly go over the steps of chest tube insertion.

The trauma room at UNM is prehistoric and quickly becomes crowded. There are larger janitor's closets at other hospitals, but this is our home and we crank out more trauma than many larger facilities. But this gives me about two square feet to set up my chest tube and one more to wield the scalpel. I am squeezed between the railing of the bed and an oversized garbage bin when the gurney rolls in. It is surrounded by three men and women in yellow and black flight gear. I call them the Pittsburgh Steelers. I grab the chest tube equipment hanging on the wall. Laurie Ann counts and the story begins.

"This is a 44 year old female who was the unrestrained driver in a rollover accident just east of Gallup. She was found at the side of the road with a GCS of 12. Her blood pressure was 169/94 with a pulse in the 120's, breathing at a rate of 24 and sating 92%. She has a head laceration and an open fracture of her right femur which we splinted. En route she has received 3 liters of Saline . . ." and it would have gone on but at that moment the woman shouted, "Where's my daughter? How's my daughter?"

One of the Pittsburgh Steelers steps back from the gurney and over the heads of the crowd makes a thick line with a single finger across his throat.

I think to myself, "Maybe this is just a football game and he's the referee." I push forward in the crowd, and plant my two chest-tube feet next to Crystal. But the more the nameless lady repeats herself, the more it becomes clear that no chest tube is needed, and Crystal tells me to start writing up the H&P. Back to the difficult intubation cart, the rusty tool cart, my desk, my place at the stinky foot of the bed.

"Hovercraft, are you getting this?" Geoff yells. "I want to read it after you're done."

But honestly all I can think about is this lady's daughter being scraped off the road.

"It was a brand new Ford Thunderbird," the lady is saying to herself. "I just swerved to avoid something in the road. Where's my daughter? My daughter?"

If she had not been tied down to the long board with a cervical collar around her neck and a splint on her leg, I believe she would have got up and walked out. "Where's my daughter?"

But all anyone can tell her is we do not know, that there has been no call to transfer her to UNM.

The orthopedist comes in. A more anatomical splint is placed after a heavy dose of Fentanyl, and then we are off to the CT scanner. All she has is the broken femur. She will need surgery. That leaves us out of this case. Ortho will take over. I am given the task of sewing up the head laceration.

By now the crowd has filtered out leaving only an ER tech, a nurse, and me. It is strangely quiet. The laceration is about four centimeters and extends from her hair line down to the bridge of her nose. Looking at it, it strikes me that this lady, whose name is Jane, will have a scar to mark the occasion.

"How are you?" I ask as I place the sterile towels over her face to isolate the wound.

"My leg hurts, but I wish I knew how my daughter was. Where is she? I don't remember seeing her after the accident," she whimpers.

"I wish I knew, but I don't," I say.

I throw the first stitch, bringing together the most recognizable paired segments. After that it is a matter of dividing and conquering and keeping my stitches close together to minimize the scar. I feel like I am working on a memorial. I don't want it to go bad.

When it is done, I take the towels off her face, and I walk out. It is dark outside. The window reflects two of the paramedics leaning on their empty gurney.

"What happened to her daughter?" I say to somewhere between the window and the paramedic.

His reflection moves in the window, and I hear his feet as he unloads himself from the gurney. He is sucking on a mint.

"She was holding her daughter, doc."

I look at him.

7

The Leaning Tower Construction Company office is on a spread of ten groomed acres of volcanic rock, yuccas, and a water fountain. In the back of the parking lot is a putting green. The custodian is here leaning on a rake.

The day has turned windy, and Father Time can see a squall of clouds in the distance. He goes through his final game plan. The efficiency of his company's work and the quality of the tiles will be his selling points.

"'My mother would buy these tiles.' No, that was too lame.

"'Unparalleled quality: tiles measured, leveled, and grouted.'

"'Not dirt cheap, but then again, you wouldn't want dirt.'

"'Parallel tiles,' Christ," he is reaching and realizes he must stick strictly to his $467,000 proposal, read from it, right down to the lien.

He straightens his tie. The door breaks open and his feet hit the pavement. His tie blows over his shoulder, but his suit stays straight. As he enters the walkway, he notes the water is being blown out of the fountain so he takes the cement to the left and looks up at the brown tinted glass rising four stories high with Bank of America written on top.

"Hello. Leaning Tower Construction Company, please," Father Time says as he files past the receptionist. He keeps walking as he hears, "Take the elevator to the third floor." It is 9:28.

At 9:30 exactly, he is at the reception desk of the Leaning Tower Construction Company.

"Mr. Hall, have a seat. Mr. Breckenridge will be with you shortly."

Out the window, he watches the sky. It begins to rain. His briefcase is a single strap of leather. He opens and looks over his twenty-five-page proposal and wonders how his lawyer could have said so much about so little.

At 10:15 he wonders what the hold up is. By 11:00 he knows they are icing him. At 11:15 he knows they mean all due disrespect. At 11:30 the secretary apologizes. Outside the rain pours. Father Time fumes. He knew this Breckenridge was going to be an asshole from the get-go, a goddamn ski resort running a construction company. His face does not flush anymore, but Father Time feels his blood pressure rise to armpit level.

"It will just be a moment, Mr. Hall. I really do apologize," the secretary repeated.

"Your accent. You're not from around here."

"I'm from Mississippi, sir."

Father Time cannot think of anything else to say. He had been in Vietnam with a guy from Mississippi who stepped on a land mine.

He opens his proposal again, then trades it in for *Time* magazine. George W. is running out of ways to embellish the importance of Iraq, although he is not running out of ways to appear on the cover. Six kids have murdered one kid in Middle America. The economy is officially stalled, not broken. The Russians are rallying around Putin, and the Smirnoff's Ice is melting.

"Mr. Hall, you may go in now."

He opens the door himself.

Mr. Breckenridge does not look up. In fact he is talking into a two-way speaker phone.

"What do you see, Charlie?" He motions for Father Time to have a seat.

"There's a man climbing out on the south concourse ledge. Two of our men are pursuing him, but the concrete is very slick, sir. The lead man is signaling to him, but the man isn't looking back. Sir, I think. . . ."

"Now calm yourself, Charlie. Nothing has ever happened at a Leaning Tower Construction site. Are the police on the way? Let them know we would like to avoid news coverage. Clearly, we aren't at fault."

"Oh, my God," Charlie says.

Mr. Breckenridge curses and hangs up the phone. He does not have to shuffle paper to look at Father Time.

"What can I do for you, Mr. Hall?"

"It's about the S.E.D. Laboratory building, Mr. Breckenridge. The tiling contract. But if you have to take care of other matters, I understand. It's a short drive, and I drive it quite often."

"No, I don't let my projects fall behind. Let's get that straight right away if you want to work for me."

"Of course, sir. I just meant the extenuating circumstances," Father Time says, nodding to the phone, but Mr. Breckenridge thinks he means the sky.

"Yes, on a clear day he never would have made it onto the site. All this miserable rain we've been having lately."

Father Time does not know what to say. He feels as if he has walked into a psych crisis center by mistake. These are the times, he had learned in Vietnam, in which you just have to go after it. You have to forget what you feel. Everyone's heart is in his guts, and the silence is geographic. You go after it.

"You've seen my proposal for the tiling in the restrooms and labs. I know it's not dirt cheap but you wouldn't want dirt. It figures out to a 5 percent profit for my company. You in turn will have solid construction and our guarantee against any lifetime defects."

"How long is a lifetime?"

"As long as the building exists, Mr. Breckenridge. That is laid out in our contract proposal on page 24."

"I don't have time for proposals. Let's get that straight. This is a business I run. I do what the accountants tell me to do and for your proposal there is $364,000 dollars allocated, and the lifetime is twenty years. I want to be building something else there in twenty years. I want your tiles gone."

"I generally don't work like that. Craftsmanship is important to me," Father Time says, but really he is stalling for time to rethink, to recalculate if he uses a cheaper supplier like T&G tiles for the S.E.D.

building. T&G tiles generally are guaranteed for ten years, which makes twenty years a stretch. If they start crumbling, he will lose his shirt and his reputation. He wonders if he compensates with a higher quality grout if this will keep them in place. This will also drive up his costs. All at once and with so many variables, the little math he knows is gone.

"If I had known in advance, I could have brought an alternative proposal," Father Time says. "As it is, I'll have to speak with my lawyer and get back to you."

"Come on, Mr. Hall, this is business. You've got to be able to think on your feet. This is your company?"

"Yes."

"And you are the president?"

"Of course, but that doesn't mean I operate in a vacuum."

"I'll tell you what, Mr. Hall. I'll give you a break. I want you to go check in at the Marriott Suites down the road at my expense. Talk with your lawyer and come here first thing tomorrow with our new proposal. If you leave, we won't have much to talk about. I think that is fair advice."

Father Time looks at Mr. Breckenridge, but now he is shuffling papers on his desk. He reaches for the phone.

8

Geoff is waiting for me when I get back to the unit.

"Where's your head at Hovercraft? You seem so fucking lost and hesitant. This isn't a job for the feeble-minded or weak-kneed. You have to be able to haul ass and pull your own weight."

I don't know how many more clichés he will use or where this futile lecture in medical education will end, but I know he has me on edge, and I can feel the bliss of his anger. This is a complex feeling to describe but it is like a purgation, to have all of your confidence knocked clean from yourself and feel free to be anything you can muster because all you have is a shell of fatigue and anger. How many times I have felt the bliss of his anger I could never count, but Geoff is like a weird spiritual figure to me. Red hair like a flamethrower, he sends a chill down my spine. He is a paradox in neatness. Throwing expletives succinctly, using words inefficiently.

"You can't go to a code with your head up your ass. You have to bring your full attention to the forefront and bear down on the situation."

"Like a bowel movement," I want to say.

"Your brain is in the sink and it makes my southern soul sick to think if you were at that resuscitation alone. What would you have done? Tell me. Fucking enlighten me."

I draw on my anger, but can find no words safe to say. "I know I need to do better," I offer.

He smells it—weakness. "That isn't good enough, Hovercraft. I want to see you in those resuscitations at the top of your game, with eyes wide open and not thinking of some silly nursery rhyme. It isn't bedtime. It's time to go to bat and win the game. You have to use your head and your instincts. You're supposed to be a doctor."

So that is what I am supposed to be. I thought the question was much larger.

9

I am the oldest guy in the ER program. I calculated this risk a long time ago, before I started the premed science credits. Now I can only let the math play out. I'll be forty-five when I graduate for the last time. It's been a long time since I experienced my first graduation: potty training. Alpha and omega, many years separate the experiences but the desire to be competent and continent have not changed.

We all come to points along the road where we evaluate where we've been and how our lives have changed. I did this a lot more when I was younger. I used to keep all my journals and scraps of paper with quotations that struck me. Once a year at least I would take that journey into the past and feel that strange sensation of a salmon struggling upstream in the fall of the year. The native dirt of nostalgia would fill my nostrils, but it did nothing else for me. I was a prisoner in a holding tank, waiting to enter the true struggle for life.

For a long time I earned my keep as a fry cook at a coffee shop. I wasn't unhappy, but how much hash can you sling with your mind lost in a daydream? It was like being on LSD chronically. The bacon smelt good and the eggs bubbled kaleidoscopically in the butter.

For my lunch break, I would bicycle to a creek nearby and listen to it as I ate a cheeseburger and fries. I always thought the river would say something to me like when Siddhartha comes to the river at the end of Hesse's book. But this river was mute and neither Christian nor pagan god moved its lips as the water rang over rocks at my feet.

I left that job and took a job as an aide at a psychiatric hospital on a children's unit. The hospital was a throwback to the days when society settled its mentally ill in sanitariums for life. There was a dining hall and a ballroom, and the whole thing was nestled in woods. The patients could stroll out and smoke in the afterglow of the sun and into the shadows of the trees. Depression was palpable. Lip smacking was an acceptable sign of affection. The screams of the violent were rarely heard; anyway, they got Thorazine. The children's unit was different.

Separated from the main hospital, it was an English cottage perched on the hill next to the hospital president's mansion. We ran our own schedule with meals held family-style around a big wooden table. It was beautiful, too idealistic to survive in an economy that was about to explode with for-profit hospitals.

I would take these kids for hikes in the woods, show them how to skip stones in the river, and in the winter how to sled down the hills. There was a five and dime I would take them to every Saturday morning after Pee Wee's Playhouse. They would pick out simple stuff like Wiffle-ball bats, slingshots, goldfish, and candy, lots of candy. These kids weren't really crazy.

I remember one seven year old named Frankie who wanted to paint his finger nails black, grow his hair long, and be a rock star when he grew up. His Seventh Day Adventist mother would have none of it, and it was our job to fix him.

One day I went on a hike with a group of kids that included Frankie. We got lost. I mean totally turned upside down and backwards in our little woods. It was embarrassing. We stumbled in the underbrush, slick, red vegetation, with Frankie up front, guiding the branches back, and no end in sight.

Frankie pointed as he stepped out into a meadow bathed in sunlight. "There it is, eternal life."

One by one we climbed out of the brush and stood. The day tightened like Saran Wrap around us. Something held us in space and time, down to the last child. I squinted. I could only see grass. And for years since, I've squinted through the *Rolling Stone* looking for Frankie's face, to feel that spiritual Saran Wrap again.

Which brings me to my point, of course. The night is long. I've lost track of time, but I'm sitting in the break room, alone, asking myself what gives me this feeling that I have lived and that Geoff isn't right.

It isn't because I have become a doctor, nor is it because I was a nurse, an aide, a unit clerk, a fry cook, or a professional Kool-aid attendee. This question has long been debated among philosophers. Was it the experience with the child herald Frankie in the meadow that made me real? Or was it when, like Nietzsche, I murmured "God is dead"? Did Descartes' "I think therefore I am" have any effect? No! What made me real were my children. I had the luck to be at home with them in their early years. My wife worked.

There can be nothing more lonesome than childrearing. I was twenty-eight when I had my first, and I would go for the longest walks with him slung across my chest. I told him everything beautiful about the world. I read him *David Copperfield* while he lay clueless with his NUK in the crib, and then we'd walk again, and I would smoke with him asleep under my chin while drinking coffee and reading a fat Russian novel at the Oriental drugstore. Then we'd grocery shop and we'd run into my wife Melissa's grandmother, a short Hungarian peasant whose family had fled from Mad Ludwig's taxation to Ellis Island. Her eyesight had deteriorated over the years, and she'd ask me to reach things down off the shelf for her and never know it was me. And I left it that way. I loved her dearly. Then it was time to go home with our sacks slung in the stroller through cold and snow to do the wash, change a diaper again, feed, and smoke a cigarette in the stillness of the screened porch. God, it was cold. The porch overlooked two alleys worth of garages that reminded me of Monet's haystacks. I always wanted to paint them but never did. I smoked while I tried to figure out how to live and how you could express the experience of life.

My second child came, a girl. I called her Birdy because she chirped and cooed in her little nest of blankets and stuffed animals. Now there were two to pack up and take for long walks. The diaper changes doubled, and my quest for meaning went on, like the cigarettes, unfazed. Now one of them was usually up. My oldest son I called Painter, and he would catch me smoking and say, "Daddy what you doing?" I couldn't explain.

Painter and Birdy were my life. We started going out every morning for pancakes while Melissa slept. We called it the Pancake Place but in actuality it was Milwaukee's greasy spoon—George Webb's. Painter would stand in the booth and knock glasses to and fro while playing with his toy trucks. It drove the waitress crazy, but what did I care? The pancakes, which I used to cook in my fry days, dripped with butter and syrup on our tongues. It was heavenly. It was our morning. Nothing else was doing. Nothing else was going to happen unless World War III came.

The place was permeated with smoke and all shades of mental illness. There was a former Green Bay Packer defensive end who frequented the place daily like us. He was schizophrenic, the gentlest man, and he was king as far as putting coffee and cigarettes away. I couldn't keep up with him. The competition, nonetheless, was brisk. This was in the days before smoking had become a moral issue as well as a health concern. Painter came to understand what his daddy was doing. He was smoking like all these other crazy people. And we were happy just to be together at the pancake place amidst trucks and spilt water. And the waitress, when she wasn't calling Painter a monster, called the Bird Brittney or Brianna no matter how many times I told her her name. She was convinced I had white trash in my car seat. But like Rodney King hoped, at the pancake place the white and the black trash got along.

10

The trauma pager goes off again.

26 yo female. GSW to the chest. CPR in progress.

Now I will get my chest tube. I run into Crystal in the stairwell. We say nothing. Put on our gowns, shields, and gloves exchanging only glances. I love her but will never get close to her.

"This is a 26 year old female who was doing cocaine and heroin with her boyfriend when they became involved in an argument and gunfire ensued. Upon our arrival she had a weak pulse which we subsequently lost en route. CPR has been in progress since with 100% oxygen per bag valve mask."

"1, 2, 3," the ER resident counts.

I wait for the word and watch as the ER resident Adam stares like a gator down her throat and passes a tube into her. Chest compressions resume. Geoff is working on a large central line in her groin when the ER resident says there are no breath sounds on the left.

"Get started, Hovercraft!" Geoff shouts.

I gown up like a priest preparing to say mass. Instead of with incense, I bless her chest with betadine.

"Hurry up, Hovercraft," Geoff says, but it sounds like a whole chorus is imploring.

I lay out the sterile towels. I am nervous. I can feel the adrenaline in my fingertips.

"Hurry up, Hovercraft!"

I am once removed from being the virgin of chest tubes. I go over the procedure in my mind as I count through the shiny instruments. I will use two of these devices but have been given ten. Why? There are two reasons for the other eight. 1) To confuse and 2) To procrastinate. You can lift them up and clunk them together like you are really doing something. Really you are putting off sealing the scalpel to the skin.

"Hurry up, Hovercraft!"

Her left breast rises under the picnic towels. I lay the scalpel against her skin and cut deeply, hurriedly. I pick up the curved forceps and begin to probe her side.

"Harder, Hovercraft. Like this!" and he points to his hip over his central line.

I lock the forceps against my hip and thrust into the outer space beneath her left breast. I cannot see where I am going. I am simply going. I am tearing through layers of muscle. Suddenly, the resistance ends and there is a rush of air.

Geoff can hear it and smiles. "Put your finger in. Hold the dike."

But he does not know I am not the little Dutch boy. I stick my finger in her side and feel the warm lining of her lung. I reach back for the chest tube, load it on the forceps, then begin to slide it over her rib. There is a hang up, then it goes forward, and I wonder if this is how Thomas felt in Christ's side, in starts and stops.

Blood and air fill the tube, and someone hands me the suction. I connect my tube to the suction tube. This connection will be taped and re-taped. No one will say it is not taped. I sew with 1–0 silk, dress with Vaseline gauze, and seal with an ABD pad.

In all the excitement I forget whether she is alive or dead. Tickle stands opposite me, but talks only to Geoff. They seem to grunt in an ancient ancestral language and nod a few times. Then everything: the person, the IV fluids, the blood, the cardiac monitor, and my chest tube lift up and move. They are going to the OR. I am left to compose another ode to a heroin goddess in the break room.

I've seen many in Albuquerque. They are young, beautiful, and you would say well kept if not for the track marks. They have kids but will cast everything aside when heroin calls, and then they will be gone for days until they show up again, sick.

I remember my first death.

I remember María Martínez María. She also was twenty-six. María had two kids separated by years of experience, nine years and eight months old. But Maria had not changed. She was down to a single vein on the side of her right foot. Nothing mattered that final weekend except getting shot in the foot. Her lover didn't matter, her son didn't matter, and her baby didn't matter. María Martínez María needed to get high. How could you explain it? It was as deep in her blood as the Catholicism in which she had been raised. It was inevitable. The thought went off and would not leave her alone until it was satisfied.

Three times Maria had gotten bacterial endocarditis and three times had had open heart surgery to replace the valves. They had told her number 3 was the last. Her parents agreed.

But it was destiny, and María never turned back. She ran away to a shanty in the North Valley. She lay in the summertime grass carefully aiming the needle into the side of her foot. She drew back a trickle of blood then laid down her burden. And that's all they did that weekend, and they didn't feel particularly good, and they didn't feel particularly bad. They were singing a song that they had sung before, though they didn't quite hit the high notes of old, but it was their song, and she knew her song well before she started sinking.

María showed up in the ER in her lover's arms one Monday morning. She couldn't walk. An echocardiogram confirmed the diagnosis. No one would touch her. She had blown her tricuspid valve. Her heart raced. She was admitted to an ICU bed. She didn't know who she was. Her only communication was to groan and recoil in pain—the two things she had desperately sought to avoid. She was put on a morphine drip and with her parents at her bedside was let go. The borrowing ended, the lying ended, the song ended. But her name María Martínez María—how could it end?

11

My third child was conceived in a farmer's field in Goodman, Wisconsin, on a beautiful blue morning. Everything was right: the oats in the field, the enormous blue sky (I was on the bottom), and the early moist sunlight between Melissa's breasts; everything except the availability of a condom. So it happened, and Iggy came along.

By now I had earned a degree as a nurse and felt it was time to let Melissa stay home. The early days were passing. I felt heaviness around my heart. I was thirty-one with no definite plans, once again at the bottom of the heap. I worked at the county hospital with the county warhorse nurses, who ran my ass ragged and flipped me the bird if I talked back. But was it exciting. AIDS had just exploded on the scene in Milwaukee and we served the poorest people. We took care of prisoners, and free men, and men who had traveled the world over. We were the dumping ground for everything no one else in the hospital wanted. The floor was 6 north. The patients just rained down on us. We were the ER's favorite destination.

I was a total nurse nerd with my white starched pants, white shoes, and blue polo shirt. I didn't wear a fanny pack. Those weren't in yet. But I drank coffee like a fiend, smoked Marlboro Lights outside whenever

I got the chance, and talked incessantly about working in the ER one day. I was told I wouldn't fit in, that they eat their young, and that I wouldn't even survive the training. Of course, I didn't believe them. I knew that they did not know who I was—and I learned that people unfortunately are terrible judges of what lies inside.

Iggy grew while the Bird and Painter leapfrogged birthdays. Iggy was an unusual child. He walked by two but refused to talk. At three he still had only used a few words, and Melissa became concerned. An intervention other than the pancake place was sought, and Iggy began his strange journey into what his father loved—language. He heard words and turned his head away. I didn't know if he was just letting his brother and sister talk for him, or he was deaf, or he simply had no desire or ability to speak.

But I had lived in a silent world as a child, seen Kennedy shot, and watched my mom go silent. Silence I knew. That wasn't disturbing. It was the absence of affection which was unnerving. Because what do you do? I'll tell you. You think of ways to stimulate yourself, which when you are young are very limited. You become self-incendiary without the aid of a single thought. How can I explain? Well, I really can't because there is no language to explain the body chemistry of wordless currents that one nurtures to feel not only real but also alive because once we get through the door into life all we want is to feel alive. Authentic. The real thing.

Then something changed my life. My mom placed me in the grass. A red ball painted with stars was just out of reach. She left me. It was a windy day, and the wind moved in currents through the willow tree in our yard shaking it up like a lion's mane. I rolled over and regarded the blue sky. The grass lay between the back sides of my fingers. It came on like lightning, a brilliance reached me. I could never be completely alone again. Call it love, call it God, or call it my Buddha nature. It fell off the vine and filled me, and I didn't know a fucking word to answer it with. I had been ignited, torched in the grass, a little over one, my mother of little use.

I can remember standing on the playground in kindergarten watching the other kids like I was a scientist doing a field study on the pygmies. I was totally objective about their play. I noted when they went on the monkey bars and what triggered them to climb off. But I could not get into my body. I waited for a blast from the heavens. It didn't come. I stood in my P.F. Flyers invisible to the world.

With intensive therapy, Iggy improved. He was still unique, wore his hair in long curls and danced like a contortionist to Matchbox Twenty, but he started to talk and stopped walking in circles around the dining room table. He grew daily. I felt like I was on the playground again watching, but this time it was my child, whom I loved.

12

28 year old female. 8 months pregnant. MVC rollover. Full arrest.

I had stolen off to the call room to just lie flat and shut my eyes and hopefully feel my body go numb. But with my thin balding head disheveled and my green eyes bleary from lack of sleep, I fling on my white coat and run for the stairwell. It is a bit like being Batman with the only vehicle at the bottom of the pole being your feet. I look for Crystal because I love her, then Geoff because hate is better than being alone, but neither one is there. I gown up mechanically, waiting, but still they do not show.

The ER resident, Dan, is putting together his intubation equipment and sticks the suction on high under the mattress. I look at the wall for a new chest tube kit, but truthfully, I do not know what I am going to do. I need Crystal or Geoff to tell me, to beat it into my head. I withdraw to the difficult intubation cart and unsheathe the paperwork needed to record the trauma.

"They're 5 minutes out by air," the charge nurse drawls like he is just saying the boringest thing on his weekly radio show.

I feel nauseous. Still no Crystal or Geoff. My palms are sweating onto the H&P form, causing wrinkles, like ripples on a pond. I start to write the little I know, "28 yo female 8 mo pregnant rollover MVC full arrest in the field." I look at it like a Chinese puzzle, trying to draw a person out of it, but I can't. It is just going to happen.

The helicopter hovers. I play the MASH theme song. It only takes 3 minutes to gain the roof, find the elevator, and make their way down. The Pittsburgh Steelers are doing chest compressions and at the back of the gurney is . . . Crystal. There is a heaven.

"1, 2, 3," Dan calls. Now she is on our bed.

"Hovercraft, take over on chest compressions," Crystal says. The Chinese puzzle opens. I feel purposeful again.

I wonder how I could be so foolish, but a human body seems so complicated and overwhelming when it is trying to die. There are really only two things to do: get oxygen and serve oxygen. I have heard of oxygen bars in Toronto, but it isn't like that.

"Stop compressions."

Dan's head bobs under the weight of the blade holding up her jaw. "I see it," he says and grabs hold of the tube and inserts it.

The respiratory therapist hooks up the oxygen. I resume compressions as Geoff swaggers into the room like he isn't fucking late and looks at me, unsure what to make of my activity.

"One of the techs can do that. Start writing," he quickly retorts.

I continue to thrust forward, now dislodging breast milk from her dark breasts.

"I told him to do compressions," Crystal says, after a pause. "There was no one else here."

"Then do them like this," Geoff says, knocking me off her chest and delivering titanic, rhythmic waves from a stool.

I follow suit.

"We're going to have to deliver the baby," Crystal said, "whether OB comes or not. Give me the delivery tray."

It is all happening quickly now. Her belly is bathed with betadine. Sterile towels fly into position. A drape is hung above her navel dissecting her body in halves: the half that clings to life and the half that is going to give birth even if death follows. I pump away on the clinging side and look over the curtain at the giving half.

Quickly, Crystal makes a vertical incision. We tear through layer after layer. I say *we* because it feels like everyone in the room is intent on the labor the mother can't give. A wail goes out like a mourning dove. Hurriedly the cord is cut and the baby is wrapped in warm adult blankets we usually place over the homeless men when they are hit by cars. There is no heater, and there is no bassinet. The ER attending holds him.

I start compressions again. The milk flows like the rock in the desert Moses struck. But now also blood starts bubbling up in the intubation tube. Soon, not unlike a great savior, she is bleeding from every puncture site and every orifice. Rapidly we are losing our chance. Atropine follows a river of epinephrine but it is all washing on the shore. No pulse returns. For an hour the resuscitation goes on. Occasionally, she moves her head from left to center, then drops back to the side like she is trying to get up and prove life is unconquerable. But she simply never regains a pulse. After an hour and fifteen minutes, we quit trying to make this mother regain her form and let a young woman be.

13

George Kennedy likes the Starbucks in Denver. It is set in a grey and green loft, strewn with East Coast newspapers. A river runs by it. And something about the running of the river makes time stop. Maddie, his youngest daughter, sits with him and drinks a one dollar cup of hot chocolate. Now how can you beat that?

In a way Judith has beat that. She elected to stay in the car with their other daughter Edith and drink nothing, which costs nothing. Judith is angry about something. George has given up guessing why and just knows he needs the coffee for the night's drive.

Maddie is perfect company, cheap company, beautiful company, simple company. George exhales then lifts an Arabic blend to his nose and pretends he is going to inhale it. Maddie's eyes widen.

"You getting sleepy?" he says.

Maddie tilts her head from side to side, measuring.

"Daddy, am I going to work in the café when I grow up?"

"Madison, I might let you wash the dishes if you're real good. Maybe even let you take the people's orders, then I'm sending you to college. Sarah Lawrence sounds like a big-girl place."

"Can I bring Bunny?" Maddie says, referring to her stuffed rabbit.

"Of course. In this life there are only three guarantees: your mother, your father, and Bunny. How'd you come up with such a clever name, anyway?"

"He already had the name." She looks at him like he is a Martian.

"A very resourceful Rabbit," he says. "Smarter than me, that's for sure."

There are no stars in Denver, and Judith is still in the van. She is not the type of woman who is going to charge in the door and tell him to get his ass in the van. She is far more subtle. She is no Helen of Troy. The thousand ships are launched, then you have to go dig Judith out of the closet because you feel so bad. At engendering guilt she is unmatched.

Sometimes it took three cheeseburgers to extinguish the self-loathing she inspired. But he did it. He ate all of them.

It is getting late. Maddie looks tired. He wants to make it to Albuquerque sometime tomorrow morning. From there, in one day's time, they will drive clear to the sea. Then he will hold Judith's hand and look beyond the ocean retainer wall to see what the seals like to eat. Yes, one day he would like to have a restaurant on the ocean.

14

At midnight I think about never going home again. Instead, I will go somewhere quiet where phones, pagers, and monitors can't be heard. I will live in a hut and grow green grass and flowers. And no one will come or go except me and the bees in our solitary glade.

The trees overhead, unbroken, as you walk up to the hut. You don't even know the sky is about to break with rain. The wooden door loose on its hinges. A fireplace and fireside table with books stacked high for rainy days like today. An ashtray with the statue of Liberty painted in the bottom of it. And I will just sit and smoke and drink coffee until Yeats's poem comes back to me: "The Lake Isle of Innisfree." Because it sounds so crisp, simple, and succinct.

I don't know if I will ever want to go back. Medicine is for dullards and extremists, and I am neither. In medicine you have to swallow the good and the bad and never talk about it. Every patient is your alcoholic parent having a heart attack, your deranged ax-murdering brother having an asthma attack, or a distant kissing cousin with lint in his navel, who thinks it is a tumor. And whether they live or die, you can't talk about it. You move on. You move on to the next alcoholic parent, day after day, but ironically things do touch you, and things do change you. And sometimes we do talk.

The moon passes out from behind the clouds and fills the New Mexico night. We are on the plaza just outside the doors of the ICU. Crystal breathes my cigarette smoke, I breathe the cigarette, while Geoff breathes his own body odor and chews tobacco.

"God that was a bitch," Geoff says, "one coming and one going. Rarely do I feel anything but poise, but this time I was almost like you, Hovercraft. My hand shook. I couldn't believe it."

"Well, I didn't notice," I say.

"I didn't shake like you," Geoff says, twisting his lip more tightly around his tobacco.

"I held the blade," Crystal says.

Quiet fills the plaza until Geoff spits.

"Sometimes I think my life is like a movie. I can tell you about scenes that have happened, but I can't tell you what it's about. And the reel just keeps going showing new scenes, more scenes, and I don't feel like I'm there. And the worst part is I don't feel afraid, not afraid of what I'm missing. I am the movie and it just keeps playing. Strange, I don't know," Geoff says, doing his best to muster the awkwardness of intimacy. "I mean I know what I'm doing when I'm there, but I don't appreciate it."

What bullshit. The truth: we are being rocked into our worst selves. We are being taught how to lie, how to be cruel, how to be arrogant and not even know it. We are being used and are learning how to do it to others. All of this is for the sake of medical education, the only way they say it can be done. A whole new generation of self-centered generals who bite with a smile and kick while they step. Very few survive the death march with a semblance of humanity. Most are too stupid to know when they have lost it. I am one of these.

We are ego junkies. We need a fix in every situation, every day. We need to be right. We need to lay out our logic and watch it glow. We need to see patients improve because of us and our decisions. We need to learn constantly, information maniacs, and if we look at our spouses, it is only so they can appreciate us, and if we don't have a spouse, we only look at the wall if two walls are willing to get together and clap in the silence of our arrogance. We are beaten and broken down the middle, and we just keep going. We can't get enough, and if shit is put on our plate, we devour it. Then we ask for more.

15

23 yo male. Stab wound to the neck. Alert.

That is all. We run from the plaza. There is no time to wipe the cigarette smell from my fingers. We are gowned and gloved in a matter of minutes.

They hit the door without stopping.

"He went out as we pulled into the ambulance bay," the paramedic says, quickly, and that is all.

He is on our bed. Geoff is at his groin with a central line. The ER resident Megan is down his throat, and the intubation tube quickly follows. No one is faster or more adept than Megan. I lift the ABD pad tamponading his neck. Blood shoots out. I quickly put it back. The trauma surgeon walks in counting the minutes. Blood is started, chasing fluids. The OR is opened and they are gone. I am left to stand around with the paramedics to get the story for the H&P. But no one knows why they are stabbed.

I break some crackers into a cup of coffee and listen.

The gas station lights glowed eerily over the Allsup's sign. The assailant came up from behind and caught him perfectly as he tried to turn away. Blood filled his fingers, then overflowed. He dropped the bag from his other hand. His girlfriend screamed, but too late. Now all he wanted was her sweet smile. He pointed to the gas station, and she understood. He held his hand more tightly to his neck and knelt down on the cracked pavement. Broken glass and broken paper cups, and he felt thirsty. How the fuck could he be thirsty? His fingers were now sticky with blood, but he thirsted.

It suddenly occurred to him that death was coming, and that he would die on the broken pavement with the broken glass and broken paper cups. His cigarettes were in his shirt pocket, but he couldn't let go of his neck to reach and light one. He was condemned. He was on the gallows at the Allsup's gas station, and he didn't have the benefit of a cigarette to pile on, to slake his thirst. He would just die.

"They're coming," Yanycell said, kneeling down next to him, too afraid to touch him. She had long brown hair and clear brown eyes. A face you could trust. "What should I do?" Her lips moved quickly, then quivered.

"I think you should pray," he said, but it was not clear to him to whom or how she should pray. There was just nothing else left. Clots hung from his fingers like beads on a Christmas tree. In the distance a siren could be heard, but there were so many sirens in this neighborhood.

Yanycell was crying.

"Come here, babe," he said with his free hand, but it was only a gesture. Now he was tired, a lost soldier in an unknown war, and the broken paper cups looked like pillows to lay his head down on. It would be that simple, as simple as sleep. "Yany what's wrong?" he said. It was all clear to him now. Sleep. Like a baby. But he couldn't seem to reach it. Yany was holding him up, and then she pressed her hand over his to help dam the flood.

A fire truck, shiny red, even in the night, pulled under the Allsup's sign. A man in dark blue jumped off, looked around, and then ran to the kneeling figure.

"Get a paramedic unit here, bravo," he said into a walkie-talkie pinned to his shoulder.

Another firefighter followed with an equipment box. A large bandage was sealed over his neck, but not before their gloves were mangled with blood. "My name is José, my partner's Bill. We're going to help you, but we need your cooperation."

He nodded.

A blood pressure cuff was wrapped around his arm. He did not move, did not listen to the numbers called out. It seemed for the first time in his life that he was scared. Life ended, even at twenty-three. But it wasn't God's fault. He wished only that his mother would forgive him and that Yany would tell her he died like a man and never begged for water until the end.

The ambulance arrived, and a paramedic took over the scene. The kneeling statue was unfolded onto a cot, and the Allsup's went back to being a secular institution for the trafficking of gas, cigarettes, and beer.

As sirens blared, he looked at the ambulance doors and thought about his life, about how he loved his little brother and sister, how he played ball off Eubank when he was young and about the time his mother taught him how to do the dishes and all the water ended up on the floor. He would give anything for a sip of water.

16

The hotel bar at the Marriott Suites is empty. The wine glasses, the brandy snifters, and the cordial glasses hang elegantly in cedar racks above a bedrock of beer mugs. The bartender is calm, bored, glancing occasionally at the large, ungainly movements of the wrestling match on the TV. Big Daddy Carlisle in a bandanna of stars and Mighty Tortuga wrapped in green foil shorts, names Father Time has never heard before, face off, go into a sweatless juxtaposition, then at the last second, when all seems lost, Tortuga loses his cool, bench presses Carlisle, and holds him aloft. Father Time looks back at his whiskey. Sheer fantasy. He looks down at his hand where his wedding ring used to be. Sheer fantasy. What is real?

He wants to tell Breckenridge off. How has he come to this impasse: to be browbeaten and told the terms of his own business? The bastard cares about nothing except deadlines and the price. That fucker had wanted to jump off his building. It could have been a fly. He was surprised Breckenridge with his crane did not come down on the man like a fly swatter.

"That Tortuga always wins," the bartender says, elegiacally.

"Another Johnny Walker," Father Time says in response.

"Tortuga is the best," the bartender comments.

"It's set up that way," Father Time says. "What's left for you and me?"

"At least we got each other," the bartender smiles.

Father Time laughs.

No one else enters the bar. At ten to two, the bartender turns off the TV.

17

Crystal and Geoff do not return for an hour and a half. When Crystal returns, she looks exhausted. She has been doing night float for five weeks, fourteen hours a day. She is way beyond desire (how could anyone desire to be a surgeon at this point?), running on animal instinct. I try not to look too closely at her after I notice the band mark from her OR cap still creasing her forehead.

"God, I could go for a cup of Starbucks," she says. "With lots of cream and sugar."

We had gone out for coffee once. Really, it was accidental. I was there on the patio, and she had walked up. I was surprised she sat down. Some residents did not look back at you.

I was smoking at the time, and Crystal wanted to know all about that.

"I can't believe you smoke, Hovercraft. My God!" It was said more in the joy of finding something out rather than a scolding, but she managed a standard line. "It isn't good for you and at your age and having gone through all this."

I was embarrassed and tried to hold the smoke in my hand when I was not puffing, but it went everywhere.

She went and got a cup of coffee and let me finish. It did not take long, and she was back.

"I hear you're from Wisconsin too," she said.

It turned out she was a child of Lake Superior while I was a child of Lake Michigan, great bodies of water you could not explain to someone in New Mexico. She was excited, animated.

"I used to watch ships from all over the world pull into the harbor in Ashland as a girl."

"There were Russian ships in Milwaukee and a circus parade, but that came by rail."

"And cold," she went on. "The wind used to break over the backs of the bare trees in the winter time. It positively howled. But the summers were beautiful, so green. Weren't they?"

I tried to agree, but I had been in New Mexico long enough to not really see the jungle greens hanging over the streets of Milwaukee anymore. The Sandia Mountains were brown, and it was that quality which let them turn pink at sunset.

"The sky was much smaller," I said.

"You have a family?"

"Yes, three kids. My wife is a nurse."

"Not me. I am alone. All those sayings about following your dreams aren't telling the whole truth."

"What do you mean?"

"My siblings are all over. My dad was a surgeon, but now he's retired. My parents live in Taiwan. My dad's Tibetan but can't go home. I haven't had a boyfriend in over a year. Doing this alone is hard. You're lucky you have a family."

I tried to feel that luckiness, but the coffee was much closer and another cigarette was needed. There was something else she wanted to say. Her lips tightened. She wanted a clear rational reason to say the next thing, but could not find it.

"Men can't make up their minds. Not really. They pride themselves on their intellectual abilities, but you have to admit you have to be a bit of an imbecile not to be able to think things through and come to a conclusion. And then you have to do it. They always forget that."

I nodded nonchalantly. Was it dawning on her? I wanted to say, "Men are always afraid. Like I'm terrified to go back tomorrow. In that silly hospital world I can control nothing, but I need it. I need to go.

So I am afraid."

"Tell me this," she said. "Why is it that so many women in medicine can't find partners? What are men afraid of? That we happen to be doctors?"

"I don't know," I said, but I wanted to add, "Maybe being a doctor can't be a happening for men. It's too big for them, even those that are doctors."

"It is such a big deal if another doctor asks you out, and doctors aren't what I would call a date, some guy quoting a study while you're trying to eat sushi. They get the sushi part but not the other."

Now I was interested. She had landed on one of my favorite words: *other.*

"What do you want?"

"Someone interesting."

"Maybe Albuquerque's the problem."

"No, I was in San Francisco before this. Actually Berkeley, then San Francisco. One real boyfriend in seven years, and he was Muslim so I was never really a consideration. He was decent, even put the toilet seat down, but that prayer thing eventually snapped him up. I was half Asian, and the other half was Porky Pig. It nearly killed me.

"We were living together, and he calls me up to tell me the news. I thought it was a telemarketer . . ."

I could hear him, the telemarketer, his English infused with Arabic, "You have won your freedom," and I imagined Crystal trying to reason her prize out of him with a large English word like *commitment.*

And then his strong Arabic: "Duty to God is all."

"What about me?" she might have pleaded.

But the telemarketer was already sliding away. "No contract. There was no contract." It was now a formality and for the first time in history the telemarketer surrendered, crossed all religious lines, said, "I'm sorry," and hung up.

" . . . I left that apartment as fast as I could. I started yoga. I became a vegetarian. I wanted to put it behind me. And then some developer bought the building anyway, tore it down and built a Gap store at the site."

I could see the day the apartment building came down, collapsing on itself, like a Zen koan, but this one unsolved, while the spectators watched until it disappeared.

"What did you do?"

"I already told you. I became a vegetarian. I did find someone else. I'm not that helpless. But it wasn't the same. I always think of Pejman, and now I'm turning into an old woman without him."

"Maybe you should scrap all this surgery stuff, get a burka, and go find him."

"Very funny," she said and smiled, but it wasn't convincing.

"There is no reason anyone shouldn't love you."

"Those days are gone. I can't run away and don a burka," she said, evenly. "I have my own life. I'm accomplishing something."

She was still thinking about him.

"That makes it easy."

"Nothing is easy," she said and touched my hand. "But surgery is in my blood."

It was in her blood and little more than a cliche. When do we ever let go of our parents and become ourselves, I wondered. Probably never. I was forty-three and still trying. Pejman was going deeper in debt to find an obedient bride. Crystal was sewing with her father. All the evidence pointed away from the concept of being ourselves. Perhaps it was just too distant to reach.

"Do you want to go out sometime?"

"I don't date married men," Crystal said. "It doesn't feel right."

"I must go," she added, noticing that I was fingering the pack. "Don't murder yourself with smoke. You're a lucky man."

But when she was gone, I did, murdered myself by cigarette, and looked to the mountains.

"No man is an island," they said. We needed each other, yet we seldom seemed to get the right amount of the other. Not enough or too much. So we ended up being an island anyway.

18

They said the snakes were out because there was a lot of rain that fall. But what was a lot of rain for snakes was hardly appreciable by human standards. The paths into the foothills were just as dry and the risk for fire on the mountain still high.

Geoff was sitting on the patio engrossed in an atlas when I walked up.

"Well, well, well, if it isn't Hovercraft come to the center of cosmopolitan culture—a Starbucks."

I had never said his name and was not going to call him Doctor now so I opted for the unpolished, "I drink my coffee black. What do you like?"

"Something with a bit of color and light on the caffeine as you can see."

I sat down uninvited, but I could tell by his breezy manner this was no offense. When he lived in Atlanta, he was kind to the pigeons. Now he was being kind to me.

"Isn't it incredible we do all these intimate things together like resuscitations, yet we hardly know one another?" I said.

"The best bedside manner is saving someone's life," he said. He went on. "You looked pretty iffy in rounds yesterday. God, you are lance-able," he said with obvious delight.

"Were you always rich?" How could I say cocky?

"God, actually you were atrocious," he laughed, then paused. He winked. It was one of his psychological tricks like drinking the Strawberries & Crème Frappuccino for color.

"I'm sorry you aren't confident," he said. "But the ventilator settings you just have to know question-answer, down pat. That's your grandma. You can't go wandering in like Little Red Riding Hood discovering her for the first time."

"I get what you mean," I lied and looked off to the Sandias. This Starbucks afforded a good view. It was right on Central Avenue and had a green screen draped over a trellis with vines for when it got hot. It had an ambidextrous fireplace with one eye looking inside and one eye looking out.

"You can't just make things up," he said. "The ventilator is a serious thing. It's life or death."

"I'm not. I'm just reading off the numbers the nurses have recorded."

I thought back to that first day I had taken Swahili in college and that whole first hour the professor had made us say 'cow' over and over—ng'ombe, ng'ombe, ng'ombe; because he wanted to get us well away from English. When I said the ventilator settings, it had the same effect, the numbers were familiar, but I was just saying ng'ombe when I needed to understand cow.

"There is nothing ambiguous about them. You have to know them," Geoff said, morally. Doctors often thought they were popes. Life at all costs was frequently their sacred ng'ombe.

It was the stress of this particular job.

"I will know them. Someday I will do my own settings," I said.

"Please don't," he said. "It might lead to a crime."

"So it's organized crime. You have to be the right person to get away with it."

"It's nothing like that," Geoff smirked. "You must simply never doubt if things go bad."

I was reminded of Plato's cave in the *Republic*. There were shadowy figures on the wall.

19

Bob Dylan was on call with us. I figured if he got an honorary doctorate from Princeton he could spend a rainy night #1 and #32 at the far more obscure and lonesome University of New Mexico. Everything I knew about Bob Dylan I learned from his songs. You could learn more from his obscure book *Tarantula* than from reading a biography by some Greenwich Village hanger-on. People simply did not know him, and I'm sure he spent a great deal of time keeping it that way. Why? He was Bob Dylan, and while you were coloring Easter eggs, he was painting his passport brown. Go figure. I could never make it out, but I liked the sound of a passport being painted brown.

He came into the call room just as I was falling asleep. I was the worn and grizzled up-all-night Doc Scrooge, and he was the bright youth leading me on a journey through the past. But he skipped right to the punch line. He was dressed all in black: black Stetson, black shirt with black rosebud cuffs, black leather pants, black cowboy boots and a long black coat; dressed the same as when he went to his daughter's graduation from Macalester and sat under the shade of a tree in back on that sweltering Minnesota day. He barely broke a sweat. He was getting ready for hell.

"Death is real," he said, rasping.

I was reassured.

The night was cold and crisp, early December on the high plains of the Southwest. We were on horseback, riding over graveyards. Dylan had a bottle of whiskey in his hand, Kentucky straight, which he poured into his mouth, not offering to share, and a pistol at his hip, not offering to explain. God, we were riding, riding so fast that we left scorch marks on the rubber cacti and tumbled tombstones littering the dry plains, and the stars trailed like comets across the Milky Way. The sky was so big and starry that to look up would have knocked you off your horse. Anyway, I was concentrating on the clopping of the horses' hooves and trying to knock Geoff and Crystal off my coattails. I was a doctor on the lam, my white coat now flannel, free of those fuckers, and enjoying every inch I put between me and them.

Dylan brought his horse to a halt and pointed to a river gleaming with star shine. "Over yonder is Mexico. I'm taking you to Juárez, El Ciudad, where the ghosts of my ancestors lay."

Then he cracked his horse again and was gone. I could see Geoff and Crystal in the distance running after me. I spat. I flew after the man in the long black coat.

I had never been to Mexico and was simply riding south looking for any hint of Dylan's shadow. I could not see but feel the two fugitives behind me scrambling through cacti and sand into El Paso. The border patrol flew by like wraiths. I was clean into Mexico, having paid 35 cents, riding as fast as I could away from duty, obligation, and everything that made perfect sense.

I could hear gunfire as I pulled past the Plaza of the Americas and kept flying, the long black coat now dancing on the wind, lit up by the festive lights, green and red, of the marketplace. The sounds of the hooves reverberated off the buildings. Still, no matter how fast I rode, in the distance I could hear the panting and see the bright torch-like hair and hear the oaths, "Get back here you lousy piece of shit. You need to update the list." And something like guilt, all misshapen and deformed, clawed at my heart, but onward I rode now looking not so much for Dylan as a quiet place to roll my bones and not be found while I counted the stars like Isaac of old.

Through a stone gate I rode, then suddenly realized I was caught. A circle of boxcars filled with migrant workers surrounded me, all chanting for freedom in Español, and the pope stood up from his high chair and yelled back at them *Silencio*! in perfect continental Spanish. Before the wind could howl, I was knocked from my horse, and the crowd roared, and freedom and silence went by the board. I could smell the whiskey and the dirt and feel the fists land all around my brain. There were no words spoke between us, he just kept coming, my boyhood hero making a mess of me. My jaw sprung loose then broke in half, and I looked at him and could say nothing. I saw Geoff next to the mumbling pope, cheering on the slaughter. For some reason I could still think even after the 2x4 exploded on my head and staggering backward suddenly remembered what William Blake had said, "But a short space/we are put on earth/So that we may learn/To bear the beams of love." The sky lit up in a flash of lightning and rain began to pour on Juárez generally.

There is a loud knock at the door that reaches into my hip. "Hovercraft, you piece of shit, get up. Hovercraft, there's a code."

I look down at my empty pager, startled. Somehow, messing with the alarm, I have turned off the pager.

And it would have been all right; it would have been all right if I had not gotten it into my head to pass the MCAT. Yes, it would have been all right if I'd flushed my name tag on registration day for medical school, burned a cigarette, and headed for home. Hell, it would have been all right if I had filled in choice B for all the answers on the step 1 and 2 exams as I planned. Landing my first choice for residency was as much a shock to me as I was to the program. That couldn't be helped. Yes, and forget all that, it would have been all right if I did not think I would stay awake if I wedged a saltine between my teeth and lips. It had formed a conduit, and I had fallen asleep in the call room like I was on a respirator.

20

I am dead in the water, dead on land, dead at sea. Dead. To think that a few moments ago I met Dylan in this brain that now feels like rocks in a butter churn on some desolate Wisconsin farm where Ed Gein is making sausage and lamps for Christmas time. Yes, I feel like a mass murderer and the victim of a serial killer all at once. I am dead, redhead dead, terrorized, but damned if I am going to take it.

I take it.

The neurosurgical ICU is ghostly quiet. All I can see is the winding of the suture knot as Geoff puts the finishing touches on a chest tube. I look in the open glass doors at a young man in his early twenties laid out, helpless, probably too dead to be alive, but this is where I am supposed to be. I step in giving myself some distance from Geoff. He doesn't look up. He hooks up the chest tube, then picking himself up off the floor lets his gaze pass straight through me. Shit, now I am glass.

Crystal, meanwhile, is securing a subclavian line, totally lost in her world, too smart to slide between Geoff and me. Here we are, three survivors on a desert island. Our raft is this young man, and whoever does the most for the raft takes the day. So strange, it must be fiction. But it isn't. I have fucked up, and Geoff just lets me feel it. No raft for me. It is the dead of night. No attendings, no administrators, in short no hospital bureaucrats on our little island. It is just us and the raft. Geoff looks at me again with that *I'm not looking at you* look, then he focuses hard.

"Have you called his parents? I didn't think so," he cocks his head, brazen with contempt, tobacco loaded in his lower lip like an arsenal. "Explain to me what you were doing. Were you practicing your surgical knot? Oh, that's right, you're an ER intern. Couldn't be that. Let me guess, you were sleeping. Well, you know, that little red thing is a pager. When it goes off, you answer it. Now is that complicated? Even an ER resident understands the color red and noise mean trouble. No, you can't ignore it. You have to rise to the occasion, which means you have to get your ass out of bed and like the little bear climb over to the other side of the mountain and see what you can fucking see. You don't lay there, little bear. You pick your ass up. You climb the fucking mountain, and you see what that fucking pager wants!"

They teach us about professionalism in medical school and then again in residency, but our time would be better spent learning how to fire up a wok. Geoff has professionalism down. I am bleeding in my pants, and I know I'm not menstruating.

"Now let's go over that again, ER resident. Little red. Big noise. Look alive. Respond. A goddamn nigger in southern Georgia could understand that." His face is distorted with rage and professionalism, then melts like a marshmallow on a hot stick. He realizes he has crossed the line, and I know that for the rest of the night I am golden.

His lips curl into a smile. He looks this way and that, then at the raft. "Shit happens," he says. "You want to put a Foley in?"

A Foley is a urine catheter. I have done it hundreds of times as a nurse. This is not a big responsibility, but it gets me onto the raft. I touch the young man's bare foot. Crystal smirks. We all act as if Geoff's behavior is not indexed in the psychiatric manual on our island. It is cool. It is normal. Nigger, bitch, cunt. We are all back to the common goal of launching the raft and making it through the night.

"What happened?" I said.

"He flipped his car," Crystal said, "on a side street. Pretty amazing."

When I finish the Foley, Geoff pulls me aside and asks me to talk to the family. It is icing. It is said in such a way that I am to derive pleasure from him endowing me with this responsibility. He fills me in on the case then. He is right behind his Hovercraft pushing me into the consult room.

A tall, thin man with greased back hair reacts to my opening the door and is on his feet to shake my hand.

"Hi, I'm one of the doctors taking care of your son," I say, shaking his and then his wife Angelica's hand. They are both in their fifties, careworn, anxious. This is probably not the first time they have been called out in the middle of the night for this son, and they are reluctant to realize this will be the last. Their duty is over.

The rest is all scripted from medical school, or so it is supposed to be. I look circumspectly over at mother Angelica and think real hard in my dizzy brain about what to say. Being a parent myself changes my perspective completely. I am not some punk Jesus telling them to let the dead bury the dead. I have to tell them that everything they think, feel, or do will now be different; that for the rest of their lives they will have to swim; that the raft is technically ours.

"So what do you know about Allen's accident?" I say.

"It's Albert. I'm Allen. I know all our names begin with A. It gets confusing," his father says.

I apologize like a librarian who has misplaced an article and keep my circumspection alive. I wait.

"Well, we know he tipped his car," Allen says, looking over at mother Angelica, "but we don't know for instance whether he was wearing a seatbelt or whether he was able to get out." Allen sounds hopeful.

"None of what I have to tell you is good," I begin and for some queer reason think about offering them coffee. "First of all, there were no marks on his body suggesting he was wearing a seat belt. Second, I hate to tell you he was found outside of the car."

I can hear the first crack in their denial break, and mother Angelica swallows. And for the first time, I notice mother Angelica has a rhythmic facial tic in which she squints in spasms. It makes me dizzy to look at her. I focus on Allen and Allen's levelheadedness.

"His head hit the pavement hard," I say and wait. "With a lot of force."

They move in their seats and look at me expectantly. God, this is gruesome, but somewhere in there I believe I have fired the warning shot we had rehearsed and been tested on in medical school. Now it comes. Now it comes stuttering and mottled with solemnity. But all at once I fail and feel my lips reluctant to do duty.

"Then he's okay?" Allen says.

"No, he's dead," I say. "Brain dead."

"He's dead," mother Angelica says, her face full of exhausted comprehension. "I knew it. I always knew my Alby would do this to me." Then she weeps in spurts, not because of her sixth sense, but because the son she bore and loved, loved against her better judgment, is dead.

It is Allen who erupts like a volcano. "O my God, O my God. . . ."

I get on the horn to the chaplain. The punk is right: Let the dead bury the dead.

21

Now somewhere in Albuquerque west of the Sandias, down on the green, between a woman's legs, the Gadfly was born. The rest is uncertain. How can you describe a mythical creature to an age that doesn't understand mythology, that has in fact turned myth into disrepute and uses the phrase, "Oh, that's just a myth." Well, I prophesy that one day we'll say, "Oh, that's just evidence-based medicine; it never made anyone's life better."

The Gadfly is different. She came out of nowhere, and where she goes no one knows for sure. She and the Go-to-Girl are the two nurses who run the *Titanic* at its most dangerous hour—night. The residents, even Geoff, are just ornaments on their Christmas cactus, and even Geoff is now in the call room merging with the hospital bureaucracy in sleep. The *Titanic* drifts, driven by the turbine of an intrathoracic aortic balloon pump. A ventilator coughs. The coffee pot lies dead with stone cold coffee. The Styrofoam cups lie on their sides.

Some people inspire things in you that no one else can. It is not for simple reasons like they are cute, friendly, down to earth, a cut above, or know more than you. Those are all things that belong to the day-to-day world, but they are not the reasons I got addicted to the Gadfly.

She is beautiful, young, with long brown hair, and a long cowboy smile when she isn't mad. She is mad often, but medicine is a world of anger. So if it was anger only, she would just be furniture, and I wouldn't have been inspired at all.

It is her inquisitiveness that gets me thinking, that always gets me looking in the nurses' lounge when change of shift rolls around. Will this be a Gadfly night? Or just another forced march till dawn? And when she is there, my heart lightens, for a couple hours I am buoyant. I am simply glad to see her and no longer care about the discomfort I am feeling. And although I can't let the patients in on it, secretly I pray, a farewell to arms.

I talk with her often, smoke cigarettes with her, and drink cherry Coke off her bedside table. She sits outside her patients' rooms, cocked over her paperwork, on guard against her feelings, wondering deep down who she is. That is why I like her, because she knows, as the Swahili speakers will have it, life is a safari, a journey, and with all the poverty one feels, that sucks. Sometimes you want to simply arrive and pierce the journey to the wall. Some people seem able to stay put, seem able to extinguish the longing, and have no regrets. She can't. There is life or suicide.

The Gadfly is alive. And I am there too, no longer looking at the *New York Times*, but staring face to face with the Gadfly. No coffee. A thought comes into her eyes and spins and spins. Then her almond eyes become distant like she is thinking, "All the friends I ever had are gone." Queer, how the night is. It passes like life yet nothing is more ancient or primal in our souls. So why fear. In fact God walked into a dark room, never said it was bad or good, before he said, "Let there be light." The night is ours. Every human being can have night in a meadow, in a ditch, or in the gutter of a call room. The night is the great equalizer, the great giver, the great substance more palpable than gold. It sticks to us. It haunts us. It makes us think of things better left unsaid. And it propels us. It opens us. It makes and finishes us. We breathe the night and it fills our lungs and brains. And poetry and myth collide and are reborn in the break room that night. I watch her move. I watch her move in perfect iambic pentameter. And I smell her—orange blossoms mixed with lime. It is New Mexico after all.

Her nickname goes back to ancient Greece, to a man named Socrates who strolled and polled the youth with weird stuff like, "What is virtue?" He was called the gadfly because when he bit into your side he never let up. Because he sought the truth by questioning everything, he was considered a gadfly, a horsefly. In short, he allowed no rest from the burning and itching of life. He was sincere and probably teasing. We have only Plato to tell us. Every time they answered his questions, he polled them again, helping them to refine their thinking until their statements were so fine, their virtue so sure that Socrates could pick it up and flip it over. Oh well! Then the next youth, whom Socrates probably wanted to screw before he returned to his wife with the long nose and pock-marked complexion, would chime in that virtue was born out of the goddess Aphrodite. And though Socrates liked his answer, even admired it, the game resumed, the dialectic continued because his integrity was at stake. He was the gadfly, the festering horsefly who would never let anyone rest content that he was in possession of the one and the many. No, life always eluded us. It was never what we thought it was. When we said it was this, it became partly that, then all that, then perfectly nothing. Oh my God. And he would talk crazy-like about Forms, Ideas, and Being-as-such. And the youths would lay down in the rubble and listen to this strange man speak, their breaths taken away, while Plato with his pompadour took notes furiously and pulled on a piece of lip that was no longer properly joined to the rest of his mouth.

This would go on until night came and it was time for the torch-light race to honor the goddess. Then Socrates would take Telemachus aside and question him on the nature of love. And they would walk out of town along some lonesome road while the festival played on behind their backs. It was the dialectic that Socrates craved, the giving back and forth of ideas.

It was this idea, the dialogue, that the medical establishment grabbed hold of and bastardized. When an attending took you on the long lonesome road and asked you about congestive heart failure, he was not asking you what you thought or what in your experience it meant. No, he was saying, "What am I thinking?" and if you could not guess what he was thinking or worse could not think at all because he was breathing in your space and starting to salivate for fresh kill, you were fucked and the slaughter began. At that point you could only let it happen and pick up your mangled body for the next round because rounds went on no matter how distorted your left ankle got or how hysterically you cried, "I can't breathe. I can't breathe." Bloated with anger and disheveled of facts, you went on. Congestive heart failure . . . no one even remembered why it was brought up.

The Gadfly is different. She questions you on your patient management because she wants to know what you are thinking. She wants to know why the postal clerk who had fallen off the dock, broken his leg, and developed a clot is now dying of massive hepatic hemorrhage in Bed 7, and whether since the clot was superficial, he should have been treated with warfarin at all? And if you don't know, you don't know. You might be stupid. They let stupid people into medical school too. The water still flows around the *Titanic* and the coffee is still brewed even if Hankie never rises up onto her swollen ankles and brews it.

But that doesn't mean she leaves you alone. She wants to know what you are going to do about his potassium, magnesium, and phosphorous and which you are going to correct first and why, and why if hypocalcaemia causes a prolonged QT interval you do not give calcium as aggressively as you give magnesium to ward off the French fellow in the pointy shoes and bells, Torsades de Pointes. And if you don't know, you don't know. Go back to bed. The *Titanic* rolls, maiden voyage and all, and Hankie never rises to discover the posterior in posterior or the brewed in brewed coffee.

But since you are just sitting there, minding the foggy ruins of time, she wants to know if there isn't something we could do for the Navajo man in Bed 9 who is spinning in his restraints on maximum doses of Fentanyl and Ativan. This is a luxury liner after all, and the man really doesn't need to row. Yes, you say, but you really don't want to paralyze this man who thinks he is Charleston Heston in the middle of *Ben Hur*. You just want to slow the drummer down. So you say, "What do you suggest?" because you know the Gadfly is way ahead of you, it is her ship, and you are just a lucky cabin boy who she smiles at occasionally for no particular reason. "*Morphina*," she says with Latin manners, as she rises. And you are left to ponder her inscription that is tattooed across your senseless evening-into-morning brain. *Morphina*. And if you don't know, you don't know. How the hell did you get into medical school anyway? The *Titanic* glides, and Hankie is strapped down to her captain's chair even though it isn't execution day, and the only electricity that needs to run, needs to run through the coffee pot, and she won't do it.

The Gadfly's skinny brown eyes and long brown hair look at you. There is a youthfulness and a transparency to her skin that in the early morning hours forms a mirror, and you want nothing more than to breathe on glass.

But this is residency, Geoff's sick fairy tale, and suddenly a large, bitter nurse is at your other elbow.

"What are you going to do about this gas?" she says massively, exploring the place between your eyebrows.

This one requires all your thought and both eyebrows. You have to put the pH together with the pCO2 then account for the bicarb without forgetting oxygenation. It is hard at first, confusing at first, and now it is the middle of the night. But the key is always to be resourceful, play dumb, be generous, and call for help.

"Let's call Bob," you say.

Big Bob is the respiratory therapist. Bob dwarfs this nurse and makes her play elephant to his T-Rex. Though there is something savage and ugly in playing T-Rex, there is something beautiful. We are all fascinated by it. Bob has crossed over that threshold to where fat becomes magical. Everything you take for granted like getting in and out of a car, Bob has turned into a master's feat. How'd he get into that Honda Civic? you wonder, and you want to watch him do it again and again.

Bob always has an idea. The lungs are Bob's bread and butter. Usually it is as simple as turning the rate up or down on the ventilator. Sometimes it is increasing the PEEP. More radically you can go from a volume mode to a pressure mode. But if you really want to surprise everyone in the morning you go to BiVent. Jaws drop. Dander is stirred. BiVent is the newest breathing technology that maximizes oxygenation, and because it is new, people hate it. I don't think one way or the other about it. I am still mourning the loss of the typewriter. And really, how the ventilator cycles doesn't concern me.

Bob eyeballs the gas through his bifocals. "Shit," he says, then steps through the sliding doors to check the ventilator settings. "You are at 100% FiO2 and you really are pushing the lid on your PEEP."

Having started with a good word like *shit*, Bob proceeds to lose you. PEEP has a lid? But isn't BiVent an exaggerated PEEP with the lid torn off? Then why the lid? You put this to Bob.

He weaves a brilliant tangle, after all this is his bread and butter, and everyone has got to look good someday. But now you know you must plunge as the large nurse pushes you closer to Bob. You stand between two titans on the brink of history. Geoff is going to kill you, but he did say nigger.

"Bob, I think we should try BiVent," you say.

The Gadfly walks by doing poetry in the corridor. The sun is coming. *Ecce Homo.* Behold the man.

22

I call Fivehead to meet me for breakfast in the cafeteria.

With three normal older sisters, Fivehead grew up humble. He grew up in Nebraska reading Willa Cather's *O Pioneers!* dreaming of ruggedness and vastness. He did not touch Plato's *Republic*. For the ignorant like me, Plato was a source of fascination during my early twenties. For others who were only competent to understand modern science, he was an object to be overlooked and forgotten. Then there were those like Fivehead who had such a strong sense of their place in the universe that it simply never came up. Plato was that farmer down the road who parked a bunch of white Chevrolets in front of his house and talked to no one, never, end of story. Go see for yourself.

And sure as shit they were there: white Chevrolets splattered with mud and rain and stinking of gasoline and gin, and when you got down under the oil pan you understood that Plato's *Republic* couldn't exist. Only a Methodist Jesus could fit under that engine. Fivehead was baptized with water in a little white church and baptized with oil under a two door Ford Granada.

And so it was.

On the day Fivehead was baptized in a little white clapboard church at the edge of Plato's wheat field, Nixon flew his helicopter out of the grass of the District of Columbia. What the significance was of dunking the one while airlifting the other, I can't say, but Fivehead had his Nixon where I had my Kennedy, at the back of his mind. The saga of bigness illuminating the saga of smallness, and somewhere out of the front door we emerged: one in front of the Texas School Book Depository and the other on a grass so special they called it a lawn.

The first words out of Fivehead's mouth are, "The record's not broken." It is our code for TA Pizza is in the house because Pizza always likes to play. He might take you by the V in V-shaped scrub top and say his one fist was C and his other was P and quiz you on the pluses and minuses of CVP monitoring at a quarter after three in the morning. It might be on the unit or at the back of the call room, he could even be eating a sub from Dion's with the mayonnaise lacing his index finger, and you might think napkins might be a more appropriate topic, but unless the napkin could fit inside the ventilator, he wasn't budging.

Harry knows how I feel about the Pizza man, and he knows how I feel about the hash browns with the green chile sauce. They are heaven done, golden brown, dropped in a pocket of burning hell, available nowhere else in the USA. They teach a fried egg how to bleed yolk and teach you how to forget the toast.

Fivehead and I slip under a Do Not Enter sign and find a table in the back of the cafeteria.

"How's your dad?" I say.

"Hanging on," he says. "You know pancreatic cancer has no mercy."

"Ya," I say. At three in the morning I am either short on sympathy or simply do not have the words.

"I'm going home tomorrow. Today, that is, after rounds. I don't think he'll be able to go fishing. That's done already."

"I'm sorry," I say. To Fivehead this is a big deal, for compared to me he had had that Norman Rockwell relationship with his father, and the *Saturday Evening Post* was a silhouette of reality. But even Norman Rockwell did not know what to do with the death bed. Nor did Fivehead.

"I'm going to see him."

"Ya," I say, but it is like a reality neither of us can envision: just being sons looking at fathers.

Then Fivehead suddenly sits up and draws a circle on the table. I have the hash browns half way to my mouth when I hear the familiar cadence of Pizza talk.

"Hovercraft, how are my patients?"

"Fine, I think," I say, dumping the load of hash browns and pull out my list to look over. There are a series of boxes of things to do. Most are crossed off.

"No one dying? No one you have questions about?"

"Not that I can think of."

"Then you're not thinking," he quips. "I'm going to ask you about BiVent in the morning."

"OK," I say, but now look doubly hard at my boxes on the list.

Then still sharp as a tack, he takes off to play gin rummy with the sailors and toothless wenches below the deck of the *Titanic*.

Now the hash browns taste like paste.

23

Suddenly, I think of the list, and the filth of dread is upon me. The list is the surgeon's Ark of the Covenant. It takes three steps to beam updates to the stone tablets that house all the information that is printed on the list in the morning. I can never remember the steps so all my updates are routinely lost into personal email throughout the hospital. No one has ever seen the stone tablets themselves, except the mastermind behind the surgery department, TA Tickle, and he has only shared them with God himself.

The list is a summary of all the patients in the trauma ICU. Pertinent items like names, medical record numbers, medications, allergies, injuries, studies, and daily events are recorded in an ongoing dialogue between the residents. It is meant to contain a summary of everything that has happened to each patient while hospitalized in the trauma ICU, and it works, and it guides. But the list is also another recipe for intern angst. Fuck up the list, and you're fucked. There are many ways to do this. The first, most obvious, and gravest is to hit the delete button. I've done it. I didn't grow up with that button on my typewriter. It's tempting to touch. Another is not to add key events, the sin of omission as the Catholic Church coined it. Everyone did this. It is human but still punishable. Next is not to have the list published, stapled, and neatly stacked on the counter when the fourth-year surgery resident bursts in in the morning, angry at life and mad at death. Or lastly and my favorite is to delete, forget to update, and not have the list ready. This is cause for death on the plaza.

My job at this strange hour, which marks the end of the night, but also its continuance, is to make breakfast of the list, put it out with a steaming cinnamon roll, and fire up the coffee. But really I don't feel like doing that. I just hit print then I staple and neatly stack, and with not a soul around, begin to pre-round.

There are twelve patients to see. I have three.

The first is Mr. MacGregor, the postal clerk who misjudged the end of the dock while toting a load, fell to the pavement, and found the mail on his chest before he found his leg. He took to bed, beer, and Dallas Cowboys games. He followed NFL football and the war in Iraq in the *Albuquerque Journal* and lost track of time. His kids still hated him, and anyway they drank too much themselves to care, so when Mr. MacGregor developed a clot in his broken leg, no one was sorry. No one was sorry except for his wife, who smoked in the kitchen but could never put together that Coumadin and warfarin were the same thing.

He took his Coumadin religiously with Lone Star beer and yelled at the television when Tony Romo fumbled in the final seconds. Another season lost. The disappointment seemed almost overbearing. A fucking chip-shot. Iraq paled in comparison. *Fallujah* was not a word you could get your hands around like Tony Romo's neck.

In the morning he would go out onto the patio and chain smoke amid the rock garden pegged with yuccas, the *Albuquerque Journal* opened to the blue sky above and his watery, blood shot eyes below. The mourning doves moaned on the rooftop and made him feel uneasy. Everyone was watching. He was watching. His nerves clicked, and his hands jerked as he read. He didn't know when it was coming. A dove moaned, his head cocked back in alarm. The sky swam with blue blisters, then something popped. He collapsed.

The second patient I call the second coming of the Wife of Bath. Everybody is waiting for Jesus's return, but I have in fact found the Wife of Bath, and in my book you take what you can get whether salvation is attached or not. She lies in Bed 10. She is a stripper who was knocked off her donkey, tied up, and beaten before she was left for dead at the top of the tram.

The tram is Albuquerque's second claim to fame after the balloon fiesta. It takes you from five thousand to ten thousand feet in fifteen minutes on one continuous cable. By day the Sandia Mountains glow with dry rock and evergreen at your feet. You might see a bear or a mountain goat. At night the Albuquerque city lights twinkle at your outstretched hands. The would-be killer had used those hands and the twinkling lights as a weird background for torture. But he did not know he was dealing with the Wife of Bath, and her story must always be told.

She was found under one of the green observation benches, her mouth stuffed with a clot of snow, her body barely clothed. The blue of the snow and the blue of bruises covered her body. Her wrists and ankles were bound with tape. She was cut from chest to thighs repeatedly, her face for some reason spared. The park ranger who found her was a former EMT. He wrapped her in a blanket and just tore down the back side of the mountain.

She had arrived in the trauma bay severely hypothermic and confused. Death was all but certain except she was the Wife of Bath, and her toothless smile half frozen, half liquid moved deeper in degrees Kelvin than you or I. She was intubated, and central re-warming was started with a new device that re-warmed the blood as it passed through the femoral vein. The chaplain prayed at her bedside. A woman who had recognized her in the paper came in and danced some concoction of Pueblo and Grateful Dead rag doll aerial. It was quite a scene, upset more than one nurse, the ventilator acting as dance partner for one and as green-eyed confessional box for the mumbling padre on his knees. By day three she was extubated, high on Fentanyl, and certain to live another day to torture the customers at Starbucks. It was said they were even getting her donkey ready to ride down Central Avenue in festival array.

The third patient is a man who is said to have crashed head-on with a UFO outside Roswell. Truth be told, he was drunk and high on peyote and made the mistake of also driving his pickup full bore into a rock while chasing a vision which he could later only recall as blues, yellows, and greens. He had flown out of the truck, and for a moment everything was still, he glided like a paper airplane, perfect, but the rock was too big to miss, and all his peyote turned to ash and blood. They peeled him off the rock still breathing, making more work for the chaplain, who was a devotee of Saint Jude, the saint of hopeless causes. It was doubtful whether Guadalupe Soledad would live or regain human form, but despite this I spent the most time dealing with his family, who had more physical complaints than the patient. Of them Santamaría was my favorite. She caught me in the lobby one day.

"Doctor, doctor, can I speak with you?" she said, persuasively like she would tell me a secret. She said it quietly too, but it was strong like perfume.

"Doctor, I have this pain."

Forget getting in touch with your inner child. From my brief stay in New Mexico, I was: 1) convinced I did not understand my body and 2) knew why they loved the suffering Jesus. It wasn't faith, vision, or some superstitious dread. It was in their bodies.

"It starts in my stomach, doctor, then spreads like the scalding water and pours into my legs where there is such throbbing my toe nails flutter. And I don't know how doctor, but suddenly it's in my face. It doesn't make sense. Such burning I can't stand it. It's awful. And if that were all, I could bear it doctor, but it creeps into my heart and pushes the walls out like a builder was pounding two by fours in the rooms of my heart, and then I get such a headache I feel my eyeballs are on fire, and flames are pouring out singeing my eyelashes, O doctor, and the smell. O doctor, what is it? Do I need one of those scans you talk about with my brother? Can you test my blood?"

What could you say? Their descriptions of pain were exquisite, their sensitivity mind-boggling, the cure elusive, and getting in touch with the inner child suddenly more promising.

"The chaplain," I say, "is a devotee. Try him."

24.

Near Springer, New Mexico, the Kennedys stop for gas. George turns off the van, which wakes Maddie up. Judith and Edith slumber on. They have been on the road for two days, and even George has to admit he is getting tired.

"Are we there?" Maddie says. "Are there seals?"

George looks around dark, deserted New Mexico. The first streaks of dawn can be seen in the distance. The only thing lit up is the gasoline pump.

"No, they are still asleep," George says. "You should be too."

George loves to travel, loves the fresh air, loves the romance of the West. If he could go anywhere in the world, it would be to the western United States. He collects postcards of Billy the Kid, Sitting Bull, Chief Joseph, and any other personage who stinks of the days of bank robberies, hangings, and Wounded Knee. He sees himself as a driver for a Wells Fargo stagecoach, someone good and honest in a place that could erupt in lawlessness at any moment.

Ever since they crossed the Missouri River, he has noticed the change in the smell of the air. There is an old soul smell to the West like it alone could introduce you to the gravest mysteries. Life just comes at you without the dissembling of tradition, religion, or governance. There is no experience factor in the West. It is only coming at you once. You only get to go through it once.

George walks in to pay for his gas. He asks about breakfast spots along the highway. He throws a Krispy Kreme donut pack on the counter, then gum and a candy bar. The clerk smokes and talks.

"Two hours down the road, there is a place called the Range."

When he gets back to the van with half the mini donuts gone, he is surprised to see Judith up and behind the wheel.

"Did you want coffee, dear?" he asks, his throat caked with flour.

"No, I'm all right. You know I like nothing in the morning."

"That's back in Jersey. I thought maybe while you drove."

"Oh no, I'm the same everywhere."

"But smell the air, darling. Why even Edith might start singing." Then he made the mistake of talking about the old soul smell.

"I think all this driving is making you crazy."

"Maybe. What do you smell, Judith?" he says, deciding to be practical.

"Gasoline."

25

The hour has finally arrived. The sun is out, her rosy fingertips ungloved, like in Homer's epic. The team assembles, some as fresh as daisies, like Lego, our blonde Scandinavian pharmacist, others looking more like roadkill some prairie dog had done mouth to mouth on on Lomas Boulevard. I am definitely of the latter variety, still sporting my wrinkled green scrubs, smiling vaguely, a semiconscious look in my eyes, my breath only as good as the coffee I drink, and my Jolly Rancher cherry red. We line up around our lieutenant, a fourth-year surgery resident named Hector who goes in for the chew more than Geoff, as he pulls up one X-ray after the next of our intubated patients. It is no time for sleep. Hector is fast approaching the time when he will be an attending. He is quickly developing appreciation for the startle reflex.

"Hovercraft, what do you see?"

"Sir, that is an intubated patient without a pneumothorax whose tube is in good position 3 centimeters above the carina with small bilateral pleural effusions whose cardiac borders are well defined and has no sign of an opacity or infiltrate. He has a right subclavian line that looks a little shy of the superior vena cava, a left-sided pacemaker, and an nasogastric tube which passes below the diaphragm. The only thing I can't see, sir, is his Foley catheter."

My fellow interns giggle, Crystal looks to see if it is okay to laugh and quickly decides it is not. Everyone else is frozen like this is the gathering planting the flag on Iwo Jima. We all stare at the computer screen. The flag unravels.

"And where are the leads of the pacemaker, Hovercraft?" Hector says, sharply.

"One is in the atrium and the other is in the ventricle." I know full well that Hector does not know a damn thing about a pacemaker.

"Are they functioning?"

"I beg your pardon, sir, but a pacemaker is an it and not a they."

"Are they functioning?" he persists.

"I don't know what you mean, sir. The leads are in the atrium and ventricle. It's a dual chamber pacemaker, and the leads appear to be well placed."

"Are they functioning?"

"I don't know, sir. I would have to look at the rhythm strip."

"Exactly!" Hector blasts, a little too loudly for this time of the morning.

And then he teaches us around the stone tablets that you cannot appreciate from a chest X-ray whether a pacemaker works, and we awe and marvel like druids, then go on to the next.

"Elijah, what do you see?"

Elijah is a surgery intern who wears his yarmulke faithfully. It dances with all the colors of New Mexico on his curly black hair.

And somehow the authority in Hector's voice evokes something biblical, and all I can see for the next five minutes is Yahweh riding in his chariot across the vast blue chambers of the sky, and Elijah stuttering in his shepherd's clothes, too breathless for words, but using them nonetheless. Is it God's chest X-ray we are looking at? I do not know. All I know is my daydreaming is about to become more intense, and all I can do is what Larry the former ER resident has told me to do, which is FHO—fucking hang on.

"OK, Stephanie, what do you see?"

Stephanie is an ortho resident who, like all the ortho residents, seems to have it exceptionally together. They have no use for Larry. I do not know where the Ortho Department gets their residents from, but I am sure it is called Together Land, and Lewis Carroll, the English pervert, would be able to tell you more about their childhoods than I could. They are never ruffled, never tired, and never overwhelmed. They smile like Charles Manson's children through tragedy and simple splinting. I would give a hundred dollars to know what juice they drink.

"This is a chest X-ray, Dr. González, which is partially rotated as you can see by the misalignment of the clavicles."

I am ready to barf, but I also admire.

"The tube is a couple centimeters high. I will write an order to advance it two centimeters," Stephanie said, "if that is all right with you, Dr. González."

Hector nodded.

"There is a chest tube on the right, and the trace of the pneumothorax is still present, but he has not had an air leak in the past 24 hours and he has had less than 100 cc out, so I think we can pull the chest tube today."

"I appreciate your management skills, Stephanie," Hector said, looking at me oddly. "But just describe the X-ray for now."

And she did. She did it beautifully like it was a Van Gogh, and the sternum was the vase; and the ribs, tubes, and lines were the stems; and the Cryptococcus was the flowers. I could see flowers surrounded by a dark horizon. I blinked.

"Geoff, what do you see?"

"Sir, it's a portable AP chest X-ray . . ."

And I listen as the coffee maker coughs thick steam, and I swear I can hear the sound of a stream in the caverns of a forest, ringing down through the smallest pebbles before pneumothorax trips me up, and I realize Geoff is diagnosing a patient and not the muddled glass of my stream. But those trees are tall, thick and green, and the pine scent battles with the coffee scent for the corridors of my memory. "Why a goddamn nigger in southern Georgia could understand that," I hear again as I look into Geoff's sterile face, and I suddenly remember.

The headlights of the pickup, like a tunnel, made out the highway framed by the evergreens. My father's deaf friend Lamont drove, a beer in his hand. Before crossing from southern to northern Wisconsin, just outside of Green Bay, we had stopped at a liquor store and picked out a case of beer, each. I preferred Hamm's, the beer from the land of sky blue waters, whereas my dad had picked out Budweiser as he was

already in his fuck Wisconsin, fuck the Packers mode. Lamont picked
out the cheapest and then loaded two. Once darkness came, conversa-
tion was limited to my dad and me. Lamont, who read lips, was left to
think with the headlights and remark about an occasional deer that
lifted its red eyes to the road. We could say nothing to him, and my
dad and I just hung on as our speed increased under the influence of
the cheapest beer.

Outside of Goodman, Lamont suddenly veered across the highway
onto a dirt road.

"Where the hell are you taking us, Cranston?" my father said as
the truck bucked and shot through the night. "We aren't going fishing
now, for god's sake. I'd bait up my goddamn thumb."

And his mouth loose with the wonders of the night, Lamont
explained in detail every rock that rolled along the side of his deaf
world. We dodged branches above and ended up in the basement of
holes. "Igneous."

"Goddammit, Cranston, what are you doing?" my dad said. But it
was futile because Lamont couldn't hear, and all we could do was brace
ourselves as he drew a second wind out of the engine. The night went
from color to a rich black and white at shutter speed. I had been in for-
ests before, but never had I seen the skeleton of the night.

"There's a pneumothorax on the right side and a chest tube that
looks like it's in the middle fissure."

Hector explodes, slamming his fist down on the desk then point-
ing at the screen. "Who left that tube there? Who checked the post-
placement X-ray?"

Shit, sticky as it is, rolls downhill. Stephanie edges her way back
into the crowd and mutters something to Crystal. Geoff looks at his
soft fingernails, then moves a thumb in my direction. I look around,
first this way, then that way, then, realizing Hankie is not a doctor,
know I have to take one for the team. I could argue, I never saw the
X-ray, but it will come to the same thing. On our little island, blame
has to be assigned for progress to be made.

"Hovercraft, where is a chest tube supposed to be placed,
correctly?"

"Posteriorly and superiorly," I say, in truth not completely sure if
I should add laterally. That sounds better: posteriorly, superiorly, and
laterally.

"And where is this chest tube?"

"In the fissure sir."

"And what's it going to drain in the fissure, fissure-ness?"

"Probably not much, even of that," I say.

"I don't want to see my chest tubes empty in the morning unless they're drained. A chest tube is like a human being. It wants blood and air."

And here I thought a chest tube was a plastic thing I might come across floating off Jones Beach in New York.

"You can't miss this, Hovercraft," he says, conciliatory now, bringing me back under the banner of Hector-ness, aware like a brilliant general that he can beat up on the dogs all day long but that Achilles is still in the offing. The thing that sets a fourth-year surgery resident on edge is not appearing in control of his troops in front of his attending. You see, there is worry and angst at every stage of our training. Other than Crystal, I do not know anyone who breathes a deep vigorous breath, and even hers is not a breath of happiness. I do not know why doctors are not admirable people, but they are not. They are prisoners of their own fate as Geoff might say. They are the big bug half-squished on the patio with the ants swirling around hungry for the yellow sweet potato guts. And you can kick and scream all you want, but ultimately like Islam you have to submit to the great Allah of medicine and invite those ants into your side. It is destiny, and I guess that is why I do it because I do not want simply to live. I want a destiny.

"Crystal, what do you see?"

They never get sick of the game.

I could hear the stream again. The pickup came to a complete stop, then Lamont killed the lights. Pitch black. Our legs quivered beneath us as we climbed out of the truck. We were on sacred ground. Lamont never tired of coming here—the nigger camps. Keep in mind this was the deep north. Wisconsin—Canada—nigger camps. It seemed a paradox, not part of the American lexicon, but we were there, and black men who used to work at the Goodman lumber mill in the thirties used to sleep here because they were not welcome to sleep in town. They drank right out of the stream. They made their coffee out of the stream. In the evening they stood naked in the stream and all around whippoorwills sang. And it was this last fact Lamont never grew tired of describing. You see, Lamont was not born deaf. He became deaf, and

before he became deaf, the thing he loved most to hear, if you can imagine getting hearing down to one thing, was not the words or cadence
of another human being's voice nor the friendly acknowledgment of his
dog, nor the comfort of a train passing in the night. No, it was to step
out of his truck and with both feet in the nigger camps hear the whippoorwills sing with all the genius nature could throw forth.

Hector stands up and passes out of our midst. Geoff and Crystal
are next. There is time for coffee, crackers, and to urinate. The battle
drums are sounding in preparation for rounds, but really I want either
to hide in the bathroom or to go home.

26

At 6:30, Father Time finds his truck and is back on the Interstate. He feels disorganized and scattered like a sad sober man, but his clutch feels extra deep. No one will tell him how to run his business, nor how to run. The sun, in its mercy, is up. He does not need big contracts, does not need Breckenridge. He is free to order ornate tiles and install them in the homes of the California rich who live among the Santa Fe poor. This is destiny, even if it leads nowhere. He needs nothing.

The last car dealership fades from the side of the road. Next there is a brown casino under the shelter of the mountains, a sign for Denver, then the sky is clear. The road is open, and nothing is left but the guilty suspension of existence.

He thinks about his men, their dry labor, and their nearly uniformly rotten trucks. They wear T-shirts, blue jeans, and iron boots covered with dust and flecks of grout. And if they smoke, they smoke out by their trucks like sausage factories so he always knows where they are. For breakfast they eat the finest green chile egg plates the Pantry can serve up, and then they eat a categorical sub for lunch and work on. They are good men, uneven men, some days better than others, but they always show.

Father Time feels around in his mouth with his tongue. The tooth, which he tasted in his mouth last night, now clearly aches. He takes the next exit, drives by a rusty iron-sculpture shop, into a Circle K.

His daughter once said God is so pure we can't even see him in our fallen state. She never explained how then she was able to preach and how he should take it when she spoke. Fallen-ness and purity were coming out of both sides of her mouth, and he could only dart between the attacks because really she would only let him be her father if she conquered him with her faith. She kept talking about the seven seals, the lamb, and a trumpet blast. He did not know what to say. He had imagined something simpler, like all the men getting up off the jungle floor.

27

"Let's get started," TA Pizza says, but really it is a matter of perspective. I am on hour twenty-something, going for thirty, and have already been through this song and dance back at the beginning. I sure as hell am not going to get started. That happened a long time ago, in fact yesterday. Let us finish this bullshit would be more appropriate. But I follow the gathering pack, confident that today we really will reenact Plato's *Republic*, and I will go home with a clear sense of justice, and that I will be allowed to go home regardless.

"Hovercraft, what makes up cardiac output?" We have not even started the first patient presentation and the pimping has begun. It will be a long morning, and I feel as noticeable as if I were sitting, waving, in a purple Ford Pinto on a game show.

"I believe it is heart rate and stroke volume, but I might have to reconsider."

"What makes up stroke volume?"

I have made it through the first hurdle only to find myself back up against the wall. I struggle and my purple Pinto becomes more purple. "It's the amount of blood that fills the ventricle."

"Use your doctor words," he interjects.

What is so irritating is he seems so quick witted, smart, and facile while I am like a mountain goat that continually has to disengage its hooves to make it the next step up the mountain. What am I doing? Doctor words?

"Preload. What else?"

"The force against which the ventricle contracts."

"What is that called?"

"Afterload."

"What else?"

My mind goes blank, and I smile in my purple Pinto, but at age 43 no one smiles back. I am one doctor word short and pretty much looked upon as brain damaged.

"Stephanie, do you know?"

Christ, you can barely hold her back. She is on a bright yellow Yamaha motorcycle doing wheelies and flooring it.

"Contractility, sir, is the third component."

"Component," I am pretty sure is not a doctor word, but her smile I am sure is a cousin to a doctor word.

"Very good. You do a good job. Who's up?"

28

We are on the second station of the Way of the Cross when I realize Stephanie is bubbling over like chicken soup for the ICU soul. She knows it and does not need any fellow named Canfield to breathe it, rhyme it, or edit it. She is a master, and all you can do is stand back in amazement, and wish you had an ounce of her spring or a cent of her aplomb. An only child from Boston, she grew up on Beacon Hill, a luxury rat tunneled in next to Paul Revere's grave. She breezed through medical school as if she were sitting with a bunch of summer school kids.

Stephanie is all over us with her smiles and shy expressions. She is tying TA Pizza's pubic hairs in knots. I cannot figure out, however, the part where Jesus accepts his cross in what she says. I want to slap Stephanie with the back of my shoe and shout at her, "Station two," but she keeps on going, describing how Mr. Lemon has gone into a nose dive and how if the overnight team had not stopped his Levophed, we would be peeling his fingers from the pillows. It makes you sick to think about, those gray, swollen fingers and that fixed Captain of Death look in his eyes. Honestly, I had not checked on him all night. Geoff must have turned down the Levophed, or Crystal; but you knew it was Geoff. Geoff was a stone turner, a lover of completeness who could not sleep and could not be happy and probably made love like he was doing a word search, "Breasts, circle."

"Neuro: Mr. Lemon moved his hands for me this morning. He is a 4-T-6."

You really have to see this guy to appreciate her Glasgow Coma Scale scoring. The first number rates eye opening. If the patient's eyes are open he wins a 4. If he opens his eyes to his name, he gets a 3, and if he only opens to pain that is a 2. If he does not open his eyes at all, he scores a 1. Similarly, verbal and motor are scored. The T for verbal means he is intubated, and there is no numerical score for that category. The highest motor score is 6 if the patient follows commands, which Mr. Lemon did in this case by allegedly moving his hand. I think the pillow slipped.

But the thing is Mr. Lemon never closes his eyes, never blinks. He just lies there, his hands propped on pillows, the captain of his ship. And we are just waves moving around him. You can almost feel the water on the floor of his room. His glassy eyes laced with ointment just stare at you. The ventilator cycles like a weak engine, but if I touch the floor of his room with a single finger, I can feel the engine of the sea. If there is such a thing as Being and Time, Mr. Lemon has found it. The Glasgow Coma Scale has gone back to Scotland.

"Continue."

"So our plan for Mr. Lemon today. . . ."

Is to open his casket and pour him into it, I think.

" . . . is wean his FiO2 to keep his sats greater than 89.

"Cardiovascular: keep him off Levophed and use Vasopressin if his pressures don't tolerate that. Continue Lasix 40 mg IV every six hours.

"FEN/GI/Renal: we will increase his tube feed to 80mL/hr to meet his calculated caloric needs. His IV fluids will remain at to keep vein open. I will change his central line as his current access has been in nine days. His Foley is on day 14.

"Neuro-wise: Mr. Lemon continues to improve. We will continue to wean his Ativan although I would like to keep his Fentanyl at 100 mcg/hr to control any discomfort."

"Excellent."

"Heme/ID: we will follow his fever curve and pan culture as necessary for temperatures greater than 38.4. His crit is currently stable so

I think we can go to daily CBCs."

"You do an excellent job."

Elijah could see the bar raised. I could see the jackals gathering on the hillside, their teeth glinting in the sunlight.

29

Station three: Jesus falls for the first time.

I am up, talking about someone lying down. I feel the asymmetry. I like to lie down when I talk about people lying down. I remember Socrates lying down, friends gathered round, as he pondered the raised cup of hemlock in his outstretched hand. That is how we are except TA Pizza raises his Starbucks cup with the funny green mermaid with a crown, drains it, chucks it in the wastebasket, and says, "Continue."

"This is Mr. MacGregor. He is a fifty-year-old man who fell off a dock at work, fracturing his tibia, subsequently developed a clot for which he was treated with Coumadin, and was admitted after he developed hepatic hemorrhage.

"Overnight events included a transfusion of four units of PRBC and four units of FFP. He is more awake, nodding to questions and following simple commands. I think he needs a Psych consult, sir. He seems awfully depressed."

"And how is the psychiatric going to talk to him while he is tubed, Hovercraft?"

"Well, you always say we should do what needs to be done even if it can't be done."

"Such as . . . ?"

"Like calling a Cardiology consult even if they can't stress or cath the man in his current condition."

"This is different," he sighs.

"Deaf people use sign language. I'll just tell them he's deaf."

"That would be lying."

"But it would sound good: a deaf intubated patient, desperately depressed. They'd rush right over."

"The only time a psychiatrist runs is when a psychotic patient is chasing him; otherwise they can barely get up enough velocity to walk. Now stop it. We are not getting a Psych consult until he can talk but probably never while he is on my service. By the way, do you know the composition of normal saline?"

I am onto this game. After having miserably failed the Lactated Ringer's test yesterday, I had a feeling he would ask me about a different solution today, and he does. He wants my ass. I gnaw at him. My hesitancy annoys him.

"I believe its 154 mEq of sodium and chloride each."

Even the way I talk with my "I believes" and "Wells" and "It could means," drives him crazy. He is a man of action. He cannot stomach the indecision. As a matter of practice he only eats salmon, a strong fish that can swim upstream, and never partakes of flounder which only stays at sea.

"Continue," he says, now annoyed.

I feel my nerves begin to crank like a bicycle chain going on and off its teeth. At any moment the chain might sag and go limp. Then what will I say? The jackals move closer.

"Cardiovascularly . . ."

"Start with Pulmonary."

"Pulmonary: he remains on volume control at a rate of 12, an FiO2 of 40% with a PEEP of 5 and a tidal volume of 450."

"Is that how you present his settings if you want people to think you know what you're talking about?"

I look down at my preprinted form. I have read the numbers exactly in the order that they have been printed, skipping nothing, and changing nothing. Obviously, the form, when it was sent down from the stone tablets, did not consult Shock Trauma Live. But they were the stone tablets.

"You need to group oxygenation, and you need to group ventilation, no exceptions. Now for the second time, what represents oxygenation and what represents ventilation?"

I try to think, but it is all coffee grounds and no water. I try to dig up a distant stream. I try to dig up a nigger camp so that I might fold my body over John Henry's broad shoulders like a morning glory on a trestle. Then all I would have to do is turn toward the sun and open.

"Oxygenation is represented by rate, FiO2, and PEEP, I believe."

"Why rate, Hovercraft? Why would you think rate? It's absurd. Rate is a property of ventilation and so is tidal volume. Two each, that's all you have to remember. Now what are they?"

I say them, but I am not confident I understand them, and that is just too fucking bad.

"Continue."

"Cardiovascularly: his pulse has been between 75 and 125."

"Why'd you let his pulse get so high? You were giving him four units of blood. Didn't it occur to you he might be bleeding, that he should be in the OR?"

I want to tell him about the *New York Times*, that I am concerned about the four women in the red scarves, and am worried about our loss of direction in Iraq, and about how the coffee pot is slowing down, probably lime, and about the crackers, how there aren't enough kinds, but never has it occurred to me that Mr. MacGregor was bleeding to death before my eyes and for that I am sorry.

"Well?"

I know I have to take it.

"I don't know if you realize it, Hovercraft, but this is not a babysitting job. You are here to think, to read, and to act."

He totally forgets that there are diapers to change. It is a bit like babysitting.

"Sir, I did not think about it."

"Luckily, I spoke to Crystal and Geoff about it. They felt if we continued to correct his coagulopathy we could avoid the OR."

"Oh."

"Continue."

"Well," I say, but now I am like a man off his horse and there is no time to remount. I just have to walk him and wrap the reins around my fist. "His Levophed is at 2 mcg/min."

"What have his pressures been running?"

"They have been running 95 to 135 over 62 to 80."

"Good."

I walk the horse, embarrassed now that I cannot ride. "His Vasopressin has been off for two days now."

"Good."

"FEN/GI/Renal: he received several boluses of normal saline totaling four liters. His maintenance continues to be normal saline at 125 mL/hr."

"Why are you running saline for a maintenance fluid? What did you learn in medical school? Where did you go?" Actually, he never said that last part because great as he is, he had gone to medical school in Mexico, and there is no literature for sore subjects, until now.

"I learned normal saline for intravascular bleeding and repletion. Lactated Ringer's for burns and pregnant women, and D5.45 with 20 of KCl for daily maintenance."

Maintenance. It sounded like a job I might be better at.

"Not bad," Pizza says, reasonably reassured. "Then why the normal saline, Hovercraft?"

"Sir, I don't know. It was an oversight."

"Continue."

"His tube feeding is at . . ."

I don't know how I make it the rest of the way through the presentation, but by the end my horse is thirsty too.

30

Station four: Jesus meets his mother. Harry, the urology resident, is up.

"Who is up?" TA Pizza is calling, annoyed until Fivehead stands to the forefront, then he smiles.

"What will it be this morning, Harry?" he says over his bedside table as if he is a bartender serving eye-openers.

Fivehead is always serious. This morning is no exception. He makes no analogies nor deviates from his script except to cash in hard science, physiology, which he learned in the first year of medical school and never forgot.

But if he were to make an analogy . . . well, never mind.

"This is a fifty-eight-year-old woman who was involved in an MVC on December 6 sustaining a traumatic subarachnoid, a manubrial dislocation, a left scapular fracture, multiple comminuted rib fractures, and large bilateral pulmonary contusions who overnight continued to require maximal vent settings and maximal sedation. This is hospital day 6 and post-op day 5.

"Pulmonary: her mode is pressure control with the following vent settings: Fi02 100%, PEEP 20, rate 14, and peak pressure of 30. Her morning gas is: pH 7.27/pC02 54/p02 65/HC03 18/and 02 sat 86.

"Cardiovascular: her rate has been between 114 and 154 with intermittent periods of A-fib. Her pressures have stayed between 150 to 205 over 80 to 96. She is on a diltiazem drip at 5 mg/hour and a Cardene drip at 10mg/hour.

"FEN/GI/Renal: her electrolytes this morning are sodium 145, potassium 3.7, chloride 102, CO2 16, BUN 9, creatinine 0.9, glucose 108, magnesium 2.1, ionized calcium 0.9, and phosphorous 3.0. She has D5.45 with 20 KCl running at 95mL/hour based on weight and her Fibersource is running at 40 mL/hour. Her ins and outs show a positive with 2435 in and 2120 out.

"Neuro: she is a 2T6 with a Riker score of 3. Her Ativan drip is a 3 mg/hour and her Fentanyl is at 125 mcg/hour.

"Heme/ID: her morning CBC showed an H&H of 10 and 28 with a white count of 7.6 and platelets 466. Her liver enzymes were stable and her INR was 1.08."

All this time Pizza is writing his note, and we stand.

"Assessment and Plan: this is a fifty-eight-year-old female status post MVC six days ago with a stable subarachnoid hemorrhage, manubrial dislocation, left scapular fracture, multiple comminuted rib fractures, and bilateral large contusions who has shown no improvement in her vent requirements to date.

"Pulmonary: I think we should consider changing to a different mode. I have been reading about BiVent, and I think in her case we could improve her oxygenation while lowering her PCO2."

"I'm writing the check now," Pizza says.

"Cardiovascular: I'd like to add amiodarone to control her rate, and I'd like to increase the Cardene to its maximum of 15 mg/hour. I'd also like to do one of Dr. Y's xenon scans to determine if she needs the high pressures to perfuse her brain or not. If not we need to be more aggressive in lowering her pressures this far out."

"Consider it done," Pizza says.

"How do I write for that?" I say, hating to hear myself break the positive gaze Pizza is giving Fivehead. The Pizza wrinkles, and I see anchovies where I should see bright eyed pepperoni.

"Xenon head CT, and I want you to read back the orders before you submit them to Hankie."

"OK," I say, trying to turn the attention back to Fivehead, my hand sweating around my pen.

"FEN/GI/Renal: we will supplement her potassium and calcium and continue her fluids and tube feedings at their current rates until a metabolic cart is done on Monday. I would suggest diuresing her with Lasix to keep her negative as needed. I calculate that she is eight liters positive since admission."

"Excellent," Pizza says because it is. Only Fivehead can stand like the proverbial head in the jungle and see the whole universe, or was the saying something else?

"Neuro: I think we should give her a Versed holiday and see if we cannot wake her up more, aim for a Riker of 4, but I will continue the Fentanyl at its current rate.

"Heme/ID: Change her CBC to every 24 hours. I think we also need to decide not to anticoagulate her. Otherwise, she has no other issues."

Fivehead is done. Fivehead is still serious; still he is not pleased. He is a urologic giant pondering fate. How can you not love Fivehead? If he made analogies he would say, "This could be my mother," but he never makes analogies.

"Why shouldn't we anticoagulate her, Hovercraft? She is going in and out of A-fib?"

There it is, taunting me. I pick up my pen from the orders I have scribbled. I know the potassium, but I want to ask Fivehead how much calcium she should be given.

"Ah . . . me?" I say. I know there is an entire litany of saints why not to give the clot buster tPA and a much shorter list for simple anti-coagulation. Why not heparin? You can give it to pregnant women. It must be good for everyone. Then it strikes me: head bleed. It is so obvious, it makes me nervous.

"She has had a head bleed," I say.

"And what is the criterion for head bleeds in months?"

"The last two."

"No, six. And if we were to anticoagulate her, what would be her annual risk and lifetime risk?"

I have to figure out a way to slow him down. I could remember Dr. Killgood going over this very topic on butcher paper with me in medical school, and just as quickly it had fled before the butcher paper could be rolled off the examination table, cut, and thrown in the basket. Dr. Killgood knew I had not listened, he had drawn the coagulation cascade scrupulously, otherwise I would have asked for the butcher paper to hang on my bedroom wall. I did not have the heart to tell him only Dylan, Jesus, and Plato made it there. Everyone and everything else I would see in the streets. I wanted a clear mind and Melissa's earthenware bones.

"Hovercraft?"

I have that stupid look in my face, my gaze like pickled sheep eyeballs. I can feel the sweat starting to run backwards and drip into my gut.

The question is opened to the general public, and the takers are so numerous that shame is inevitable. Only Fivehead does not speak, and everyone knows he knew the answer. So it is just me—a frog in the road, and the big truck goes squash. I wrap my intestines around my forearm and go on.

Fivehead comes up behind me and briefly puts his arm around me. That is Station five all by itself.

31

Station six: Veronica wipes the face of Jesus.

Lego has been silent for most of rounds. Occasionally a pharmaceutical question is directed at her, and she has to stand up and perform like the rest of us, but she is on full salary.

I always imagine Lego is married to a rich industrial tycoon, but there is no industry in Albuquerque except the Sandia Labs. We are still the government's hideout. The world's largest nuclear arsenal still overshadows the tennis courts where Lego plays. They are called the Four Hills and lie upon the land like four plucked turkeys which have had the guts cleaned out of them and then have been stuffed with bombs. They baste in the sun like bad billboard signs which you eventually ignore.

"Lego, what do you think about Cipro for this man's bladder infection?" TA Pizza says, acting coyly. He never tires of engagement. He will fight with anyone, even the cafeteria ladies over what constitutes a well-done cheeseburger.

"Ian, your disagreements are legendary," Lego says. "I think Cipro is fine in this case. It's highly effective against gram negative organisms which is the most likely source."

"But fluoroquinolones cause resistance not only within but outside their class. How can that be good?"

"That isn't good, but in a controlled environment like the ICU where you know the patient will complete his course of antibiotics, it's very unlikely to occur."

"I'm not buying that."

"I'm not selling."

"I'm right."

"Well, I'm not wrong."

This is our republic so far—blonde and beautiful and argumentative to the teeth but allowable because she is outside the class system of medicine. But inside it is about governance by a mysticism of power. Rasputin runs rounds and we, the fledging medical mystics, nod. Like glass charms we try to reflect him back to himself. Ultimately, Lego loses. We fuck Wisconsin. We fuck the Packers. The man is started on Zosyn, which is the Budweiser of the ICU. That is that.

32

Station seven: Jesus falls for the second time.

You would have thought Jesus was a stumbler if you followed the Stations of the Cross. He falls an amazing three times. Approximately a quarter of the stations are of him falling. Falling must mean something, but what?

And now that he is down again, I am up and so is Guadalupe Soledad, the peyote mystic who bought the rock. Pizza is brimming with a malicious confidence. In short, he is ready to kick some ass, and I know it will be my robin's egg ass.

"Mr. Soledad is a forty-six-year-old Roswell mystic."

"Stick to the pertinents, Hovercraft."

"A forty-six-year-old male with multiple facial fractures including a Le Fort 3."

"What is that?"

"It's a complete fracture through the orbital floors, separating the facial bones from the cranium."

"How is it fixed?"

"I don't know."

"Look it up. Continue."

"Bilateral hemopneumothoraces, a fractured dislocated right shoulder, an open-book pelvic fracture, bilateral comminuted femur fractures and blown knee caps."

"Use your doctor words."

"Bilateral comminuted patellar fractures.

"Overnight he continues to worsen."

"Just the pertinents."

"I think doing worse is pertinent."

"No, it's not. You need to give the specifics."

The sun was already up over the river by the nigger camps. I thought I saw an eagle through the tall pines but it might have been a vulture. I rubbed soap on the bottom of the coffee pot and set it on the fire. I breathed and thought, "Freedom soon will come."

"His chest tube drainage went up. His trach sounds like a harmonica and his crit is singing the same old same old—give me blood."

"No. No. No," he says angrily. "You need to use your doctor words. Somehow you seemed to have outwitted the stupidity of the cheat sheet, Hovercraft."

I keep going. To go back involves more peril than I care to involve myself with.

"Pulmonary: he is on volume control with a rate of 12, a PEEP of 15, Fio2 of 80%, and tidal volume of 450 cc."

"How is oxygenation and ventilation presented? If you knew what you were doing?"

"Separately."

"Yes, and how is that?"

I have been up all night, save an hour, but it could be worse. I could be in Iraq yelling out doctor words to a dozen determined insurgents who don't know doctor words. We live so small, thinking only of the language that has our currency, but as human beings we have the opportunity for much more. I grew up under the rigidity of nuns in habits who used Catholic words like *original sin*, and now I was doing it again. True, the trauma attendings thought they were smarter, more elegant, and cooler, but really they were frustrated nuns who wanted a stake in that pure pleasure of hating children.

"Hovercraft!"

I hear the ruler whistle through the air. "Oxygenation is Fio2, PEEP, and rate."

"Not again. Tell me you did not say 'rate.' Tell me you know rate is a function of ventilation."

"Honestly, sir, I don't know what it's a function of. It could just as well be a function of the soda machine downstairs. Cokes per hour, that's something I understand. I grew up in restaurants. My mind was fresh back then, now I'm tired and I can't think of, for the life of me, how to get a quarter into that ventilator in Mr. Soledad's room so he keeps breathing."

"Hovercraft, Hovercraft," he says, grabbing his temples. "Who let you in?"

"A very nice man on the fourth floor."

"And you understand you're not here to be either a poet or a fool?"

"I know. I was hired as an ER resident."

"Don't explain it to me. Continue."

"His gas this morning is a pH of 7.22/C02 52/P02 60/HC03 16/ and an 02 sat of 90%."

He lets me go on, down the lattice of cardiovascular, FEN/GI/ Renal, neuro, and heme/ID. I am down at the bottom of the wall. He is Juliet leaning on the windowsill of his bedside table. He picks at his eye. He has totally tuned me out. He picks at his other eye. I am fucked. I can move my lips all I want. I am talking to a wall: Juliet Pizza, blonde-haired nun. I had never realized how bad it was to be Romeo down in the dirt.

33

Station eight.

The nigger camps were beautiful in the summer. You have to understand there were no monuments, no iron bell, nothing to write graffiti on. It was a place and a spirit all in browns and greens with a believability I never felt at one of those prescribed historic sites. The people here had struggled. I never could get enough of their ghosts.

We made coffee on a makeshift fire, then we walked a mile down-river through the woods listening to white-throated sparrows. At Dunbar Point, we entered the river. Lamont sought out the deepest holes, whereas my dad and I liked to keep the water below our knees. The fresh scent of pine was everywhere. Lamont was in heaven. Stream fishing was not a talking sport. Besides, Lamont swore the rainbow trout could hear. Now I never saw ears on a fish, but I obeyed because I liked to think they could hear the rush of the water as they swam. My dad, on the other hand, was like the town gossip in the middle of the dense wilderness. He talked from the moment he entered the stream until he tipped into the stream after his eighth beer. In Packer country, he talked nonstop about the Chicago Bears and how bad Miller beer was. He had opinions on everything, but as Socrates would say, he was not a lover of wisdom.

My dad was a lost soul. As I struggled through adolescence, I watched him disintegrate. He could not, no matter how much alcohol he drank, pull it together. He made excuses why not to go to AA. He made excuses why not to work. He could not deal with having a boss so he went to church instead. Jesus just laid there and looked at him. Jesus was not the kind of boss who told you what to do. He did not give annual reviews. Really you could pretty much do anything you wanted, and he was there for you. So my dad went to mass in the morning, then said mass again at a bar in the evening. All walks of life came to hear him speak. He was known for his television homilies in which he would pick out one TV in the bar and let it have it. His rum and coke trembled in his hand as sweat found new wrinkles to drain down. He beat George Bush, Sr., black and blue. He took on the Ayatollah Khomeini, Pol Pot, and Hitler all in one breath. But what most thoroughly agitated him were conspiracy theories surrounding the assassination of JFK. It drove him crazy. For some reason it was like making Kennedy die again for him. He would have been institutionalized if he were not so drunk. He would drink water aggressively afterwards to dilute the blood of Christ rushing through his veins. Then he would come home.

He started talking before he hit the door about something that he had heard on the radio, and he did not let up. He grabbed dinner and ate himself to sleep in front of the television. However, the alcohol paradoxically made him sleepless. By 6:15 he was back on his knees like an aborted fetus trying to get out of Limbo.

Today he thought he would talk to me about sex for the last time. Kind of like a parting gift. I was eighteen. But what he did not understand was that intimacy started a long way before sex. I needed to trust him, and I did not. I needed to be honest with him, and I could not. I needed to respect him as a man, but he was not all there. Yes, most people would see a man there because they expected to see one, but those of us who knew him saw that his legs were cut off. He hobbled on his knees. Try walking around on your knees for a while, and you will see what he was up against.

Historically, the discussion about sex had been an exchange of phrases. The first had been after my fifth-grade Sex Ed night at school. The monsignor had closed the meeting with the mysterious admonishment: "My little friends in Christ, you must not waste the seed."

As soon as we were out of the parking lot and onto Waterton Plank Road, my dad pulled to the side of the road, clear into the gravel. Our red AMC Pacer idled around us. We were like two fish in a fish bowl. I was trying to figure out what the seed was. What I did not know was the long association between gardening and sex. I did not know John Milton had said that a woman's body was like a garden. I did not realize the garden of Eden and nakedness intertwined around knowledge, and that I was on the brink of discovering the seed tight against my underwear in the middle of the night.

"Have you thought?" he said.

"Thought what?" I said.

"About it?"

"The seed?"

"Sort of."

I did not know what to say. He clearly expected me to lead the discussion.

"What is it?" I said, my voice gone hoarse like a man's, my hands full of sweat and the dirt I had played in that afternoon.

"A mystery."

"Like a hero with a bad guy?"

"No," my dad said. Then the word came, so strange in my father's mouth that it was like a single shot out of the book depository. "A cosmic mystery."

I did not know what to say. Cosmic was something after death. It was Kennedy's head going forward then back. "So the seed is cosmic. Then there is no chance of wasting it," I thought.

But my dad was way ahead of me.

"Sometimes you have to waste it just for practice."

This was new territory. The only thing I remembered about the Garden of Eden was that God got mad. Like an alcoholic parent, he came storming down into the garden demanding an accounting for every seed. He breathed life into us, he seemed well pleased with us, well contented enough, and then he got mad and chased us out, poor homeless folks for all eternity. You could not get more decisive than that. And the angels locked the gate and kept guard with torches. I could still see it: their feathered wings filled with muscle, the torches in their talons. And we were in the dark, and the joy of our lives was now wasting seed just for practice.

I looked at him, half darkly, waiting for more, but there was no more.

"Any questions?"

"No," I said softly.

"Good."

The AMC Pacer stood erect and roared. The stones at the side of the road that night gathered no moss. We were back on the road like two guinea pigs racing down Waterton Plank.

My dad's last sex talk was more complicated. I asked him straight off what the seed was, for old time's sake. He busted out laughing. He never said.

Station eight: Jesus talks to the women. Not exactly where I wanted to learn my tips for hooking up, but you get what you get in this life.

34.

Station nine: Jesus falls for the third time.

I duck my head into the Wife of Bath's room and just watch her breathing, struggling, in the dark silence, and know that death is coming round. I rarely have feelings about such things. I am not an ICU savant, nor have I developed judgment other than to expect that half the people will die, their lungs like broken rubber bands, and their pulse dumped out like mercury balls. Then it is time for the death packet and the summing up of last things as an institution proclaiming death. Willa Cather's *Death Comes for the Archbishop*. We never wrote a death packet like that, but we shared her bare contours and austere mannerisms. It is death and death only. Death so naked you can feel the slipperiness of life as you zip up the body bag.

"Who is up?"

I poke my head back out. "I am."

I can see his disdain, old-fashioned like percolating coffee—bubble up, bubble down. He does not know whether to bite my head off at the outset or lure me into a trap and let my lungs saw away. He has a bullet of crackers. He is watching me, spreading me like cheese on his crackers. Up goes the whip and out comes, "Continue."

"This is Usher Doe, that name's fake because we don't know her name, a twenty-eight-year-old female who was assaulted and left for dead at the top of the tram. Her injuries from head to toe include an unblemished face, a contused trachea, and a right broken collar bone."

"Doctor words," he barks like a dog that has drunk out of the cesspool.

"Fractured clavicle. Fractured ribs four through nine on the right and ribs 3, 5, 7, and 8 on the left. She has extensive bilateral lung contusions, a lacerated spleen. Bilateral inguinal hematomas and a right tib-fib fracture. Her torso and legs are covered with lacerations. She could not walk. She fell, and he kicked her under a bench."

"We've all read the paper. Stick to the pertinents."

"Overnight, the patient was re-intubated and sedated on Fentanyl and Ativan. She is not doing well."

"Present, Hovercraft. Stick to the presentation." It is all annoyance now. He has drunk a Boost power shake in the interim. It leaves a foul taste in his mouth, and his thirst for the evidence becomes more aggressive.

"We have her on BiVent, but her CO_2 continues to climb."

"What? Who said to put her on BiVent? What is her PCO_2?"

"64."

"Are you trying to kill her?"

"No, sir. I was trying to oxygenate her. I tried her on pressure control and volume control, and nothing worked. Her PO_2 kept dropping. I remembered you saying BiVent provided better oxygenation, so I tried it."

"That is insane. You should have called me. I'm definitely going to speak to your director about this."

He is referring to the nice man on the fourth floor. I feel sick, physically sick like when Curious George is threatened with, "I'll tell the man with the big yellow hat." I feel ashamed, guilty, and humiliated. I have followed every trick the respiratory therapist had thrown my way, but I ended up choking on my own vomit. I have to take responsibility for my own vomit.

"I should have called for help," I say, sullenly. I swear I can never make this medical world thing go right. I am either too timid or too reckless, and my judgment is never his nor her judgment. I would say it is a crap shoot, but craps and jacks were before my time, so it is more like Pac-Man jawing at my ass, and I can't wait to turn into a ghost.

"Did I not stop you in the cafeteria and tell you to call me any time? Any time?"

"Yes."

"Then why didn't you? You clearly had reached an impasse."

"I didn't want to bother you."

"This is not bothering me. This is a patient's life or death."

Just then, as though to prove his point, the cardiac monitor alarms. The Wife of Bath is having runs of V tach.

"Give her an amp of calcium, 4 grams of magnesium, and bolus her with 150 mg of amiodarone," he calls out sternly to the nurse, then smiles almost conspiratorially. Our best efforts are under way. "Then we'll start an amiodarone drip."

I am left, a grasshopper looking up at a billboard. The sun is hot, and my back leg itches. And I hope she lives not because she wants to, has said do everything humanly possible, or as an American simply expects to go on living to the next Super Bowl. I hope she lives simply to save my skin.

35

Father Time feels for the tooth with his tongue and massages his jaw, but now he is not sure which tooth it is. The whole right side aches like a flaming wall. This is what an abscess is, he thinks. He finds himself in the center of a cool, well-lit Circle K. They have lights everywhere. Time is here too, the ancient goddess Chronos, right next to the Heath bars, the aspirin, and the toiletries.

He might as well and with dignity hauls his four pack of Colt 45 Malt Liquor to the register. Their eyes meet only for a moment. He throws on some ibuprofen for good measure "and a pack, a pack of Camel straights." And then as though time has forgotten him, he is back in the wide open air of I-25 heading north, a child of destiny and the Colt 45. He tosses the pack of Camels out the window.

And he drives on, slugging beer with every ibuprofen he takes. He feels like one of those sacred monkeys that kneels at the communion rail and closes its eyes in utter darkness and lets those fimbrae on the tongue rise up under the host and for a moment clings to something like life itself. He swallows and his tongue jimmies up next to the tooth.

The body of Christ—who could have come up with such a monstrous thought? "For a little while I will leave you . . ." Even Christ is thinking about time and not some gypsy medicine of bread and wine. "And yet I will return."

Father Time looks at the horizon from one end to the other.

The gravel jars him awake, and he is back on the road. He pops his second beer and looks around for anyone who might betray him. But the traffic is light and flowing freely. Like linen on a clothing line he feels he can just ride the rope home. The pain in his tooth is starting to ease up, and the nature of time, as a facet of coming and going, is clarifying itself in his mind. "And yet a little while."

His truck runs all the way into the gravel and onto the grassy median. It is a fifty-fifty shot. He jerks right and is right for the last time.

The third beer goes much quicker. The horizon is getting closer and closer to his front end. It is practically up to his teeth, to the tooth which no longer hurts. He can taste pure New Mexican blueness. "What is this 'in a little while and you shall not see me and again a little while I will return.' What is this 'little while?'"

His truck swerves, bounces in the grassy median, and this time he continues his leftward course.

36

Station ten: Jesus is stripped of his garments.

Fivehead is up. Crystal and Geoff are excused to go to their evaluations. Stephanie squirms, dying to get the teacher's attention and approval even if it means being like a skunk that wants you to know it's by the roadside. TA Pizza looks at her approvingly and wonders.

Fivehead goes forward like Gregory Peck in *To Kill a Mockingbird*, laying out his case, point by point. If I had not had such a bad morning and collided head on with failure, I could have enjoyed it, or I could have enjoyed hating Stephanie. But both are impossible. I am twisted up like a Zen koan, pretty damn useless, and desperately in need of the back of the master's boot.

"So what are we going to do, Harry?" Pizza asks.

And then it happens. It is not a scream. It is not like a series of ahs following a beach ball around at a game. Nor does it go off like a gun before the foot race begins. It happens, and Hector has torn the hospital gown off the Wife of Bath's chest. He applies the pads above and below her heart, straight over the lacerations closed with black nylon. Pizza has his hand on the wife's femoral pulse. Fivehead is looking clearly at the monitor. Lego stands by the crash cart. Two nurses are at the bedside. The rest of us crowd in, dancing fools waiting for the disco balls to light up.

Hector dislodges the paddles that were docked like two ships in the harbor of the defibrillator. He lifts them and stretches out the cords. We watch Fivehead call the play by play.

"V-tach, does she have a pulse?"

"She has a pulse. Have we started the amiodarone drip yet?"

"No, we're waiting for it to come up from the pharmacy," both of the nurses at the bedside say at once.

"Then let's re-bolus her."

"Okay," Lego says.

The medication is administered in the boutonnière on her left chest wall that we call a central line.

Then she goes down under the lake like a rock. Hector does not wait for the play by play. He presses the paddles down hard, chasing her under the water.

"One, I'm clear. Two, you're clear."

All I hear is, "Hovercraft, get your hand off the bed."

37

It is all an impaction of metal until Maddie comes flying overhead. Judith cannot even put up her hand to stop her. Judith is dead, the steering wheel crushes her chest. George goes peacefully under the engine. Maddie lives a few terrible seconds then lands on the side of the road, utterly alone. A tumbleweed lurches onto her back to mark the time. Nothing else moves. It is the middle of the morning on I-25 between Albuquerque and Santa Fe. The fields around the highway stretch for miles and miles, and in the distance you can see mountains, brown mountains sprinkled with green. The sky is immaculately blue, and if you look real closely, you can see a politician on horseback, but he does not know. He rides on.

Meanwhile the traffic in both northbound and southbound lanes comes to an awestruck halt.

The white pickup truck is clear through the front seat of the blue Chrysler mini van. One man rushes to the scene, then a woman stumbles through the grassy median, her knees tottering beneath her. The man cannot get inside so he pounds on the minivan like he is waking soldiers from sleep. There is no answer. He presses his face to the glass, but all he can see is a straw colored haze. The woman kneels at

Maddie's side. The sky overhead, so massive and blue, peers down. And no one can say definitely what life is. And no one knows exactly where the sky is, but the girl with the white chalky face is certainly dead. The politician on horseback rides on. He does not know.

Then there are sirens, legions of sirens, like crows they come, out of the sky, in dark T-shirts, and quickly. Fire-Rescue. The Jaws of Life cut into the minivan's side. At first they find George pinned under the engine, stone dead, and then they find Judith looking back, back at something as the steering wheel collapsed her chest. They have to make an entirely new cut to access the back seat.

As the Jaws of Life rear back, the blue sky wrinkles and the mountains move closer. A can of Colt 45 Malt Liquor falls to the pavement. The crew working on the white pickup truck have got in. Using just a crowbar, they break open what had seemed like a safe. Dust and smoke fill the cab. There is blood, a spoonful, and a man who looks at them. It isn't a politician on horseback. It is worse. It is Father Time.

"I think we have one," the call goes out. The minivan has two rectangular eyes, top to bottom, on the passenger side, and peering out of the second eye is Edith with a bullet of blood on her lips. It is a different Edith, all unraveled and clinging to the back of the front passenger seat, her eyes locked on the horizon. Her face is broken but her arms are straight, her body flush against the back of the seat. The contortionist has gone parallel. She is a badly injured young girl.

"She has a pulse," one of the medics says and tries to ease her off the back of the seat in an attempt to extricate her. But extrication is a sticky business. In this case the seat she had stretched her arms around had acted as a compression dressing, and when she is taken away from it, blood flows from her heart to hidden spaces which only show up in the best anatomy books and you and me. Edith dies in one breath.

INTERLUDE

On a hilltop outside Athens, Plato once stood up and looked around. He was alone now. The Acropolis stood to the West, a herd of goats and sheep to the East. A seagull acknowledged him silently with his wings spread blue, a mirror of the Mediterranean. Under the bright cumulus clouds, he could think like no man had thought before, and he was conscious of this fact and realized history was standing up in him and changing. Soon there would be others, already there was the young Aristotle who he could barely stand. But how much was thought a political party or an exercise in personality? Ultimately, thought possessed the possibility of transcending oneself, however briefly, and reaching the mainland of humanity, not as a do-good-thing, but as a revelation of Being.

I drift further back in the crowd and make for the bathroom. I lock the door. I look down at my hand. I am shaking.

38

Three shots rang out.

There was the initial impact deforming the blue body of the Chrysler minivan, then the tearing shot of the engine being lifted out of its case and driven, and finally the recoil of the pickup truck as it regained the earth. It could have been Dallas, Milwaukee, or Miami. It happened to be on that stretch of I-25 between Santa Fe and my beloved Albuquerque. That stretch of the road well-traveled, slightly beautiful, a place usually so peaceful. So peaceful if you get out of your car in the middle of the night, you will see stars beyond reckoning, and if you look real closely out into the galaxy, you will see the five stars of the politician on horseback.

But here, where we are.

Three shots rang out, and all the Kennedys were dead.

39

Somewhere back there are stations eleven and twelve—crucifixion and death. Put them where you want. After all, this is a kind of self-help book.

But we are at the electrocution of the Wife of Bath. Hector, being a clear-headed sailor, never loses his focus as the trauma pager goes off. The paddles are down, and the electricity runs through. The Wife of Bath flails.

"She's still in V-tach. Does she have a pulse?" Fivehead calls.

"No pulse," Pizza says with his other hand on his hip as he scrolls through his page.

I look at my pager. Hector calls, and Hector shocks.

50's male. Head on collision at highway speeds. Hypotensive. Conscious.

It is that last word that gets me. Conscious. I hope he is not too conscious.

Pizza is thinking, and Pizza is eating himself. He will have to stay and manage the wife and let Hector go down. He is not a surgeon, and he is sure this guy has a belly full of blood. He grabs the paddles out of Hector's hands and calls for epinephrine.

"Go. Take three of them with."

Hector looks at him solemnly, almost embarrassed. He wants to let the boss yell one more time so he will not feel guilty or in any way superior to him.

"Go, damn it," Pizza yells.

Fivehead and the two dancing fools closest to the door, who turn out to be Stephanie and me, bolt for the stairwell. Hector is mad now.

"You're doing the chest tube, Harry. You're doing the line, Stephanie, and Hovercraft, you're writing," he yells, but it is like a blur. The adrenaline is so raw.

"Get the OR open," Hector is yelling into his cell phone. "Yes, now!"

The hallway went, the electric doors went, another hallway, and a fishhook turn and you were in the trauma room, the trauma bay, the amphitheater, the coliseum where no more than a dozen Romans in blue togas and eye shields could fit.

The team assembles: the respiratory therapist, the pharmacist, two ER nurses, an ER tech, an X-ray tech with one large machine on wheels, an ER resident, an ER attending, and us. It would have been a scene of mass confusion and chaos if everyone did not understand his or her two square feet and stayed within them. Then it is possible. I, for instance, am very familiar with the rust pattern on the difficult intubation cart that serves as my writing desk. I stand upright and do not move my feet backward or in any way impede access to the equipment in the cabinet behind me. Yet I could lift my neck like a giraffe because the space above is free. It could have been Africa or the last pocket of air in the sinking *Titanic*. I sometimes wave my hands in it when no one is looking just to prove I am still free, but mostly I just stare at the empty ceiling too tired to look into the kaleidoscope of experience any longer.

The cart rolls in. Everyone's spine stiffens. Then all at once the noise starts. The canvas sack that held the patient is thrown open.

"This is a fifty-year-old male with ETOH on board who crossed into oncoming traffic on I-25 and crashed head on into a van. He was awake and alert on scene but has rapidly deteriorated since we got him into the back of the rig."

"What are his vitals?" Hector says.

"Sorry, doc. His pressure was 108 over palp with a heart rate in the 120s. Last vitals: 89 over palp with a pulse in the high 140s."

"How much fluid has he gotten?"

"Two and a half liters so far and 3 and 4 are hung."

"Was there much blood at the scene?"

"No, I'd say 100 cc max."

"Why wasn't he intubated?"

"He was talking sir. We thought he was better served by scooping and running."

"You're right," Hector says graciously, but that is where graciousness ends.

"I want an X-ray now. You're going to intubate," Hector says, looking at the ER attending.

"Of course," comes back the curt reply.

"His breath sounds are diminished on the left. He's sating 85%. Fivehead, place a chest tube. Stephanie, place a cordis in a femoral site. He has a strong pulse."

Hector is alone on his icy crag, shouting like the great Nietzsche as reality pours over him.

"We need to get this guy to the OR," he says, suddenly changing tactics. The man is not improving with resuscitation. He is drowning. Hector looks at Stephanie and despairs. She is fucking around with the guide wire trying to be perfect like she is shucking Mendel's peas and history depends on her. He looks at Fivehead and despairs. Fivehead's right hand is bleeding. He looks at the Laurel and Hardy ER team intubating and despairs. They could have been playing eenie-meenie-minie-moe esophagus or trachea here we go. He looks at me and despairs. I am writing like a kite, large letters all over the page with sub-notes and illegal abbreviations.

And just when it seems like it could not get worse, time itself grows hair on the chin of a woman and out of the hair steps TA Tickle in camouflage pants, scrub top, and long white coat. Two archangels glide at his side: Crystal and Geoff. A sense of panic spreads through the crowd. We have all been school kids once and now more than ever long to hide behind each other. Tickle sits down on the opposite stretcher, bitches out a police officer who has snuck in the room then demands that Hector tell him what the hell is going on.

"Sir, we have an unrestrained fifty-year-old male involved in a head-on collision."

"Skip the bullshit. What's been done?"

"We are intubating him, placing a chest tube and central line."

"Meanwhile his pressure looks like shit," Tickle says, looking at

64/38 throbbing in red on the telemetry screen.

"Yes, sir."

"Then what the hell are you doing here?" he demands.

Silence descends. Everything goes dead except the machines. We do not breathe. We do not let our hearts beat. No one is prepared. The sky could not have grown darker, a gray cloud more damp, or the lightning more electric. All at once Tickle stands on his feet, and like when Moses descended from Mount Sinai we fall to our knees, blinded. He has the stone tablets.

Brilliant and provocative, he bears them, yet like earthworms in the middle of a storm we dare not look. We wriggle in our puddles. He bears them. The weight is crushing. How could he bear them? I would explode. All those years of basic science followed by four years of medical school, crowned now with residency, and already I have been let in. The stone tablets. I feel like a Jew when first he was new. What inscription could they hold? I grab hold of my pen. The first stone reads: Go To. In panicked cursive I write at the bottom of my H&P: go to. Go to where? Egypt? Would it be a riddle that would take years and a long journey to resolve? Already, I could see myself paddling out of Lake Victoria into the Nile, discovering the red eyes of crocodiles by kerosene torch. Fuck, it is dark and those red eyes, but go to I would, and never look back until all the mummies were unwrapped and the secret of surgery and the three steps to accessing the list were unraveled.

Tickle begins to struggle with the stone tablets as though they were two ancestral beasts. Crystal and Geoff come to his aid. A light shines. Hector weeps like only a surgeon can, that means little tears on the inside, then his lips part and he speaks what lay at the heart of the stone tablets: "Go to the or. Go to the OR. GO TO THE OR!"

I am the last Roman in the Coliseum. I watch the lions pull out of town. Half-used equipment is strewn all over the floor. I kick the needles to the side. I pick up Fivehead's chest tube, look at it, then pierce the garbage. His blood clings to it, wet, and in testimony.

40

TA Pizza is waiting for me. The Wife of Bath is dead. He does not ask about the trauma or anything like that. He simply says, "Let's step outside."

Unless you were out on the plaza smoking, it is a very inhospitable place. It separates the hospital from the library, and I am beginning to hate both places. Medical students linger there, too innocent to know these were the types of plazas onto which the French used to roll guillotines. That is why there is not a fountain. It is false plaza peace. Their day will come. Today I just watch them and watch Pizza's shadow surround my feet. I turn.

"I want to talk to you about your performance," he begins.

Reality floats in a vague form over his shoulder and up into the sky. And though it is right there, I cannot hold it. Reality is gone. It is just he and I. No mother. No father. Nothing that came before. Nothing that ever was. Everything is stripped away. All I can think is that this is how soldiers must feel on the battlefield: dead before they have even been killed. Running wide open. Their mouths dry.

"I will proceed by asking a question. All right?" he says.

I assent.

"Would you not agree that a ventilator has some end?"

"I would."

"And the end or use of a ventilator or of anything would be that which could not be accomplished, or not so well accomplished, by any other thing?"

"I don't understand," I say.

"Let me explain: Can you see, except with the eye?"

"Certainly not."

"Or hear, except with the ear?"

"No."

"These then may be truly said to be the ends of these organs."

"They may."

"Then now I think you will have no difficulty in understanding my meaning when I asked the question whether the end of anything would be that which could not be accomplished or not so well accomplished, by any other thing?"

"I understand," I say.

"And that to which an end is appointed has also an excellence? Need I ask again whether the eye has an end?"

"It has."

"And has not the eye an excellence?"

"Yes."

"And the ear has an end and excellence and does it not follow that the ventilator has an end and excellence?"

"It does."

"And can a ventilator fulfill its end if there is not excellence in ventilator engineering?"

"Certainly not." I have the McCabe nod going flawlessly to this Greek riddle. We are like corned beef and spinach.

"Would you not also say a ventilator cannot fulfill its end if there is no one to run the machine, for certainly a ventilator does not go in a room, plug itself in, and light up with the correct settings?"

"Certainly not."

"For let's say even if a ventilator could walk into a room, plug itself in, and light up, would it not also need to know the health of the body to which it was attached?"

"I would think so."

"Hovercraft, have you ever seen a ventilator walk?"

"Only in nightmares."

"So you would agree that a ventilator can't walk, plug itself in, and light up?"

"I would."

"And would you not say its end is dependent on something else, its excellence achieved through the agency of another's excellence?"

"Yes."

"And the same observation will apply to all other things in the ICU?"

"I agree."

"Well, and has not the doctor an end which nothing else in the ICU can fulfill, which belongs neither to nurse-ness or respiratory therapy as such? For example to superintend and command and deliberate and the like? Are not these functions proper to the doctor, and can they rightly be assigned to any other?"

"To no other."

"And is not life to be reckoned among the ends of the doctor, the purpose assigned to him?"

"Assuredly," I say.

"And is not life the excellence for which the doctor strives?"

"Yes."

"And can he or can he not fulfill his own ends when deprived of that excellence?"

"He cannot."

"Your excellence is terribly suspect. It is not the eighty-year-old man who comes in in full arrest or even this thirty-year-old woman that worries me, but I wonder what you will do when a two year old comes in not breathing. That you can't fuck up. You have to know what you're doing, and I don't think you do."

I don't know how a fire gets started in the human gut, but I am on fire, and perplexed. I am not even halfway through my intern year, and I am being told I will suck two and a half years from now. And yet you have to read between the lines. Pain is the best medicine. Academics were like farmers who believed unless you beat the corn, it would not grow, so out into the field they would go and drag you in. And either you became so cold that you gave up or you became so cold you continued on. It was cold on the threshing floor either way.

"Today I am going to speak with your director and recommend

termination. Frankly, I don't know what the hell he will do, but I wanted you to know my thoughts. *Pregunta?*"

So this is the failure my father always talked about. I could feel my head fall like a chestnut on the Parisian streets of old. I could hear one medical student laugh in particular like the fucking horse of a French king. So be it. I walk in with Pizza, unencumbered, like he is my friend.

41

As fate would have it, and it was fate that had me so often that first year, I run into the Gadfly in the hallway.

"What are you still doing here?" I say.

"Re-certifying," she says.

I think to ask in what, but then realize it has no bearing, and I am all into bearing at the moment. "Do you have time for a smoke?" I say.

"Of course."

The medical students are still out on the plaza, un-bagging their lunches. Good practice for being airport security if things go awry.

"Have you ever thought about what the meaning of all this is?" I say.

"All the time," she says and lights my cigarette.

"And what have you thought?"

"That it has no meaning in itself, but compared to life, it seems real."

I nod my head and tap my cigarette. I say and do nothing more than smoke. Life is passing. The stream is flowing. The nigger camp is still intact because no one knows where it is.

"But what do you think?" she says.

"That I am doing the wrong thing. That I am no good at this."

"You're plenty good," she says and touches me, not with her hand, but the dead ring of her voice. She doesn't give me that talk about not personalizing it, about forming a harder shell, or simply going home and sleeping on it. She doesn't say don't cry. She doesn't say laugh it off. The plaza and the high blue New Mexican sky surround us.

The medical students get up one by one, then in twos off the floor of the plaza. The sweat on their brows and the creases around their mouths show concern about the coming dissection. But no matter how much they study or how much of the human body they undo, their mouths will never be as naked as the Gadfly's.

AFTERLUDE

It is nearly one o'clock in the afternoon. Ian Pizza likes to teach us for
an hour at lunch. I have been in the same place for the past thirty-two
hours, eaten thirty-three graham crackers and seventeen saltines and
drunk twelve cups of coffee. I cannot take anymore. I might go home,
where guilt will stand like a potted plant over my sleeping form. The
word *termination* rolls halfheartedly around in my brain. I wish. The
bastard. My friend. I grab my bag from the break room and walk out.

Hector is sitting at a computer staring at the list. He seems
depressed, annoyed, everything but angry at the fates.

"What happened in the OR?" I say.

"He didn't make it," Hector says.

He does not look up, keeps looking at the list. I get behind him,
fiddle with my head, and try to see what he sees. I think maybe if you
look at the list long enough, you will see Plato's *Republic*. But it really
is just letters. Father Time died without saying a word, not a woman's
name, not even mom. He never made it to the list. He died with the gas
going down his throat and the knife in his belly. Won't we all?

And now it is time to go to Starbucks for cup thirteen, drink it down black, and hand out cigarettes to all the mentally ill. For like Jesus said right before he died: *Tengo sed.* I thirst.

Then they took him down and laid him in a tomb.

I will wait for him, but not for long, enough to finish a cigarette with the homeless men. His tomb could be anywhere. Tomorrow will come soon. I look to the Sandias and pick out one stone, any stone.

This stone is black, large, perched, and alone in the sunlight. It is certainly within my right to stare at the mountain and blame the stone. Everyone needs a stone to blame.

I simply no longer can.

TENGO SED

Design and composition by Karen Mazur

Set in Bell MT with Roadkill Heavy display